*"An Instant Chemistry Novella"*

I0566586

# *In Between*
# *Chemistry*

## Taylor Love

**Taylor Made Day Dreams**
Bringing an "imaginative break" to your day!

## In Between Chemistry

### Copyright © 2021 by Taylor Love

ISBN: 978-1-948383-12-7

**Taylor Made Daydreams**
www.TaylorMadeDaydreams.com

# About the Author

Taylor Love is an African American author who calls Michigan her home. An avid reader since she was a young girl, she gained a love of writing as well. Her hope is to share Sexy-Modern-Romances, that showcase mainly African American couples in a positive, real and uplifting light! She loves to read a variety of genres and hopes over time to expand her writing among several of them. She is a lover of learning a "little bit" about many things. She hopes her imagination brings readers a few hours of enjoyment!

## Instant Chemistry Series
### Running Into You
Not My Type
One Click For Love

## A Instant Chemistry Novella
In Between Chemistry

## Vacation Love Series
Crashing In On Love
Lovers Hiatus

## Instant Chemistry Shorts
Cam & Andrea-New Years Eve
Cam & Andrea-Don't Forget What you Have At Home
Robert & Mika-Weekend With The Lordes

**Stay In Touch!**
**Facebook-** https://www.facebook.com/TaylorMadeDayDreams/
**Newsletter- (No Spam)** http://eepurl.com/duB-Fn
**Twitter-** https://twitter.com/TaylorLoveWrite
**Instagram-** https://www.instagram.com/taylorlovewriter/
**Bookbub-** https://www.bookbub.com/profile/taylor-love

# Author Note

This is my 1st novella, which is a work that is between 20-39k (anything 40K and above is technically considered a novel). I'm long-winded, always have been with my emails, letters and writing, so this was a challenge for me. I'm a freestyler or as some say a panster writer as well. It's a struggle (for me) to get all the details I consider a *must-have* in under a 40k window. Since you are reading this, it means I succeeded (in my mind) in doing it justice. A big thank you to Antonio & Julia for allowing me to tell their story and open up the window for more of our favorite characters to come!

# Prologue

Sitting at his desk Antonio wondered why this hump day Wednesday felt more like dumpster-fire Monday. Everything that could go wrong—had. Like him failing to close a low-tier client signing on the dotted line. The rapidly growing business had been actively looking for a company to manage its 401K plan. While it was small money today, it had the potential to be big tomorrow. Antonio understood "you win some, you lose some" but was still pissed about it. Which was why he sneered when Robert came to his door.

"Whatever you're going to say, don't." Antonio preempted.

"So, I should keep my offer to take you to lunch to myself?"

"Since you already said it, I accept." Antonio turned to send a quick email to the administrative assistant but Robert waved his hand, dismissing the action.

"I already let her know we might be a while."
Standing to fix his tie, Antonio didn't speak again until the two were riding down in the elevator.

"You're a cocky bastard, you know that right? I could have said no to lunch."

"I'm aware." Robert was unfazed looking at his phone, not even lifting his head to acknowledge the insult. "My wife reminds me several times a month."

"Of course she does, she's a smart woman. You're lucky I didn't meet her first."

Robert only snorted at that, they both knew his wife Mika was crazy in love with him. It was disgusting, yet amusing to watch the stubborn, lustful pair together. Lately, Antonio found it hard to keep his envy from showing, he was entering that point in life where he could envision a relationship like that of his own. Most of his friends had gotten married in the last few years and he'd seen how happy they were. Guess it wasn't in the cards for him yet, because to date he hadn't found a woman he wanted to risk it all for.

*

They were at a small American-style bistro a block from the job eating a quick burger and having a drink. They didn't drink often during work hours but every once in a while it was warranted. As they wrapped up Antonio nursed his drink, thanking Robert for getting him out of his momentary funk.

"Don't sweat it man, on to the next. And no problem about lunch, we were due. Actually, I've been meaning to talk to you since last week if you've got a little more time."

"Shoot."

"I was thinking about asking Lawrence this, but since our dust-up at the end of last month I don't want to see him more than I need to."

"That's right little Bri has a man now." Knowing that his sister's boyfriend was a sore spot made Antonio chuckle. It was rare to have ammunition to needle Robert with, so he enjoyed any chance he got.

Robert narrowed his eyes. "Don't let her hear you call her little or you might get a fist for your trouble."

"It's all good, we Hispanics like feisty women."

"Yeah, whatever. Anyway, you know Mika mentors young inner-city girls at her center, well a few months ago they decided to expand it to include boys as well. Of course, Cam and I were automatically recruited and the cousins joined in too."

Antonio knew "the cousins" referred to Robert's four male family members. He'd gotten to know them over the years and even better when he was a part of Robert's wedding party.

"That sounds cool. I'm glad you guys decided to do it. Hell, young men need all the help they can get."

"Yeah they do, so here's how we're trying this. We'll have two meetings a month, one with just us and the boys and another with both groups. We met our six young men three weeks ago, but we've already signed up another four that should be coming next time. A couple of our boys are Hispanic and one of the four joining is as well. I started thinking it would be good for them to see a role model that looked like them, particularly since I know you."

"Me, a role model?" Antonio was genuinely amused. "First time I'm hearing that."

"Cut the shit Tone." Robert used the nickname he called Antonio outside the office. "You're one of the most righteous men I know, you would be a great example for all the boys."

"Awww, keep sweet-talking me, you're making me blush. I should have you phone my mother with all these compliments."

Robert ignored his jokes and went on seriously.

"These boys need stability, so if you joined that would make it seven of us. Only two or three folks need to go to the co-ed meetings, so we could rotate that. But we'd like as many of us as possible to show up for the boys-only sessions, that way we can really connect with them. Don't say yes if you can't commit the time needed. You feel me on this?"

"Yeah, I feel you."

Antonio wet his throat while Robert let him think on it. After a full three minutes, he drained the last of his beverage, looking across the table at his colleague and good friend.

"I'm in. I don't know if I'll make a difference, but mentoring will look great on my resume at least."

# Chapter One

Three days later, on the third Saturday in June found him pulling into the center's lot, and Antonio was thinking maybe he shouldn't make important decisions on the fly. Seriously, what the hell did he know about being a mentor? *He* sure as hell hadn't been mentored by anyone, not even his older brother. No male role model in his teenage years either, as his father had died of a heart attack when he was ten. Worked himself to an early grave with two jobs providing for the family, and even then he was barely able to keep them a few steps above poverty. Antonio had been determined not to live the same and clawed his way into a more lucrative career.

It was one of the things he had in common with Robert, and why they bonded. They'd been able to smell the need to succeed on each other from the moment they met. It quickly became clear their upbringings were similar, and they shared wanting to break the cycle of money uncertainty. All so they could live an easier life while having the tools to help their families. This was why ultimately he hadn't bowed out from being a mentor. If he could be a window to show other young boys that it *could* be done, or simply be a sounding board for their issues—then he would do it. Something he could have benefited from while growing up.

With that last thought in mind, he went inside greeting all the guys warmly, before turning his attention to the ladies. The shock when he locked eyes with Julia was another indication of how scattered his mind was. After all, she was one of the founders of this center, of course she would be here. Antonio had no problem with her, *she* on the other hand seemed to regard him like an annoying piece of gum stuck to the bottom of her shoe.

Trying not to let her cool gaze bother him, he studied the kids as they filed in. That, plus watching the commotion that ensued as an unknown lady walked in with one of the new boys was enough to distract him for a few minutes. By the time everyone arrived and Andrea settled them down, Antonio was thoroughly amused. Watching the teens warily interact with each other was like watching a middle school dance, everyone awkward and at the same time curious.

The meeting started and they explained the objective of these combined sessions. To teach the kids interpersonal skills and collaboration with the opposite sex, as well as better overall communication skills. Life and work wasn't just made up of one gender and they figured fostering partnerships now was a great way to teach healthy dynamics and respect for each other.

Hell, Antonio felt they should make this a required college course. There was so much discord in society around relationships right now. People killing off their spouses, instead of having the balls to just get divorced. Add in all the sexual harassment and bullying that went on in the workplace and it was clear that men and women needed to be *taught* how to exist with each other.

They did some ice breaker exercises that included not only the kids but the adults. Mika even roped the lady in the back into participating on that score. She complied, though it was clear to see she didn't like being put on the spot and left promptly after that. Since it was the first co-ed meeting they wrapped up ten minutes early and Robert took that time for all the guys to have a brief meeting with the boys before sending them on their way. Since there wasn't much clean up the adults soon found themselves standing around talking.

"This is actually happening huh?" Kimberly looked around at everyone shaking her head before smiling. "Lord help us."

"It is and I think it's great." Julia was excited. "Young men need guidance too!"

"It's going to be a lot of work steering knuckle-headed boys down the right path." Thomas complained. "I had to do it for these three," He pointed to Robert, Darrell and Devin. "Edward wasn't so bad, but now I have a teenager at home who is driving me up the wall."

"You should bring Kalen next time, he could benefit or at least set a good example for the other boys."

Thomas rubbed his chin. "You know Andrea, I think I will. We need more father and son bonding time anyway. Because in a minute I'll blink and he'll be off to college."

"Don't go getting misty-eyed about it." Robert said dryly. "That's the goal, get him prepared, hell all these kids prepared and *out* their parents home."

An unchoreographed "amen" echoed around the room at that.

"Hey, now that the rugrats are gone let's go eat."

"Darrell! Don't call them that." Andrea admonished.

"Come on! I'd never say it to their faces!"

"Knowing you I'm not so sure." Mika pinched him. "But I like your idea about getting some food. Let's get out of here."

*

They left with some carpooling to the restaurant where luckily it was only a fifteen-minute wait for the eleven of them to be seated. Antonio made a point of sitting next to Julia, who looked none too pleased. The wink he sent her way didn't help either. After they ordered and the noise rose with various conversations, Antonio turned to her.

"So, how have you been? I haven't seen you since the wedding."

Julia sighed, leisurely sipping her water before turning fully to the man on her right. "There was no reason for you to see me. I've been fine, thanks for asking."

"You're welcome. I've been doing good too...in case you were wondering."

She bit her lip refusing to smile and encourage him in any way. He'd tried outright flirting when they were on the island, and she shut him down firmly but kindly each and every time. Now she did the same again.

"I wasn't wondering."

"Shame, because I've wondered about you a time or two." He tossed back.

Antonio wasn't bothered by her light insult, it was the same as she always treated him. Even now she was looking at anything and everything but *him*, trying to dismiss him as a non-factor. Well, not today. He'd lost one deal this week, he wasn't about to lose anything else.

"Tell me why you always pretend I don't exist? Did I offend you and not realize it? Do you think I'm a complete jackass? Out of all the men sitting here, I don't even rank in the top three of that category."

"Beg your pardon?" Julia was caught off guard by his testy reply. Before he'd always responded with slick charm.

"You *should* be begging my pardon, for how you always treat me."

"Are you kidding me right now? So a woman is rude because she doesn't want to interact with *you*?"

"Of course not, just when she goes out of her way to be cold and distant. Look around you at everyone at this table. These are cool people, you've spent real time with them, shared in their life moments just like I have. You don't treat anyone else here like you do me. I just want to know why, especially as we're about to be working together to shape young minds."

Well, that had her flabbergasted. Julia just wanted to keep her distance from the man, never thought he would care and take it so personally. Everyone else at the table through her friendship with Andrea and Mika, were basically family by default. But Antonio...she couldn't put him in the "friend zone" so easily.

"I'm sorry you feel that way, but I don't really owe you any explanation."

Antonio leaned back and just stared, while he tapped one hand on the table. To her credit she returned his gaze, not backing down. Oddly he liked it, liked it so much that he decided to keep pushing. But this time he tried a different tactic.

"Don't tell me it's some obscure rule where two Hispanic people can't be seen talking to each other. I know that's a thing for black people, folks start to think they're planning a revolt or something."

Julia cracked a smile at the joke. "Don't forget I'm half black, but no that doesn't apply to us. Though, if there's three or more of *us,* someone may come over and ask if we're looking for work."

It took him a few seconds to believe she was actually joking with him before he laughed. So hard in fact a few people at the table looked their way.

"You *do* have a sense of humor. I figured you must, being friends with Mika."

Julia rolled her eyes in her friend's direction. "Mika has enough humor for all of us."

She watched as Mika gave her husband kisses while he looked like he'd rather be asleep. But Julia saw the sparkle in his eyes and knew he loved every minute of it. Moving on to Andrea, who she considered one of her *best* friends made her release a deep sigh. Her husband Camden was feeding her fries, and they were just about the sweetest couple she had ever met. He doted on Andrea day and night and it didn't hurt that he was sexy and kind. Frankly, both ladies had relationships she envied. And why was she thinking about any of that right now? Shaking her head, Julia turned back to the man next to her.

"Antonio...what do you want from me?"

"What do you mean?"

"Exactly what I said. You flirt, I turn you down and the cycle apparently continues. So *exactly* what do you want from me?"

"Well for starters, I'd like for you to stop turning me down without even getting to know me. I don't know where we got off on the wrong foot, but you're a beautiful woman and I like to think I'm a good-looking guy. It would be nice if we could have a normal conversation or two."

"That's just it though, I feel like I know enough to determine that I *don't* want to know you any better. I'm sorry if that sounds harsh, but I don't think we're compatible."

"Damn, low blow but I still think you're wrong. Go out with me just once, next weekend. We can try to get to know each other as friends at least. It will be better for all involved if we're on good terms because I don't plan on going anywhere. I promised Robert I'd be all in on this mentoring thing and I meant it. One date, we act like civil adults, have a little fun and a lot of conversation. Let's set an example for the young folks. What do you say?"

Julia narrowed her eyes, he talked a good game but she didn't expect anything less from him. "I think…you should never use the kids against me to try and get your way, but I'll bite this time. One date, civility included but don't expect much else. You plan it and let me know the details."

"Deal." Widening his smile he held out a hand.

Hesitating, Julia eventually shook it.

# Chapter Two

As soon as they'd shaken hands last week Julia knew she had made a mistake agreeing to this date. That same damn "zing" as when she'd been introduced to him at the airport before the wedding had happened again. If she didn't know better she would say it was an allergic reaction to him, but common sense told her it was attraction zipping along her nerves.

Objectively she wasn't surprised. He was tall, with shiny jet-black hair and bright brown eyes. Not to mention a smile that said he was definitely naughty but worth it. By the time of the wedding photoshoot, he'd started flirting with her, and it was a wonder her panties hadn't slithered directly to the sand. Then and there she doubled down on the vow not to be a cliche and hook up with *any* of the fine single men in the wedding. Even with their natural attraction and the free-flowing alcohol she'd somehow managed to keep her goodies to herself.

Now she was putting herself in harm's way with this date. Going out with him was *not* a good idea, and the text informing her they were going someplace semi-fancy gave her even more pause. She wasn't falling for it though, putting on a green dress that didn't show much chest and also came down to her knees. Something she could wear to work by adding a blazer, the goal was not to flaunt *anything* tonight. But she still added some light make-up, there could be someone else she wanted to attract.

Who was she kidding, she wasn't that callous to talk to another man in front of him. Honestly, she didn't want to deal with *any* man right now. Lately, Julia wasn't feeling love and love wasn't feeling her either. Hearing a car pull into the drive, she had no more time to fret about cupid screwing her over. Julia had made another mistake by allowing Antonio to pick her up, which meant he'd be bringing her back and trying to worm his way inside. It was too late now, so she grabbed her purse and quickly left, only to find him on the porch step already.

"Well, hello beautiful!" Antonio was remembering why thoughts of her randomly popped into his head, she was gorgeous. "Are you that eager to see me? I was coming to knock."

"I wouldn't say that. But I didn't want to keep you waiting either." She left out the part of not wanting him to step a foot in her house.

"Let's get the night started then."

Antonio brushed closer than needed as he moved behind her, opening the door to his cherry-red BMW Z4, causing Julia to hold her breath before sliding in. It was going to be a long night.

* * *

Antonio took her to Cliff Bells, a jazz club downtown for dinner. Folks at his company often used it with clients, so most of the crew knew him. Enabling him to get a table up front right by the stage on a busy Saturday night. He was hoping she was impressed, but it was hard to tell with Julia, he considered himself lucky she'd come out at all. Antonio had been expecting a text or a call saying she was canceling all afternoon.

On the ride over conversation was polite, general talk about work and more detailed talk about the kids at the center. But now they'd exhausted all the safe topics and he was interested to see where this would go. So while sharing an appetizer of mini Maine Lobster rolls he tried to draw her out.

"Ask me some questions Julia, whatever you want to know. That way rather than *thinking* you know who I am, you might actually find out."

"This is the part of dating I always hate." She said halfheartedly. "It makes it seem like you're interviewing people."

"I feel you, but I promise I won't take offense. Ask me anything, I'm an open book. Plus remember this is more of a "get to know you" outing than a date."

Julia tried not to be blinded by the beguiling smile he sent her way, but also reminded herself to relax. She could more than handle anything Antonio sent her way, so she threw him a softball question.

"Tell me about your family roots?"

"That's an easy one. The bulk of my extended family is from Texas, though there is a small contingent of the family on the east coast too. My parents were adventurous and moved to Michigan when my older brother was just a year old. A few cousins on both sides followed later, so there is a bit of family I grew up with but not much."

"Just the one sibling?"

"Yes, thank goodness."

Julia smiled. "Don't tell me there's at least one other person in the world you can't charm?"

"You could say that. We get on each other's nerves is all. I got all the charm and he got all the cynicism. Talking about roots, don't mock my smoothness, it's in my DNA. My people came from Venezuela over eighty years ago to the US. What about you?"

"Ahh, you have me beat. Mine came from Puerto Rico on my dad's side nearly seventy years ago. Through Florida and worked our way up the coast. We're spread a bit all over. My dad came to Michigan for school and met my mom, who's black if you were wondering."

"Why would I be wondering?" He asked, clearly confused. "I think it's women who worry about things like that. I'll tell you a secret, men are very basic. We only care that a woman looks hot, not why."

"Hmmm...a little bit shallow, but you may be right." Julia thought about his words, nodding in agreement. Most of the grief she had ever gotten for being mixed had come from other girls or women.

"Anyway, they met in their junior year of college then married three years later to the displeasure of my abuela."

"Don't tell me because of your mom's race?"

"No, there's black in my dad's lineage too, so that wasn't the issue. My dad is the baby of his family and granny just didn't like him getting married at twenty-five."

Antonio blew out a breath and took a drink. "That *is* really young."

"I agree, but when you play at shacking up and get pregnant..." Julia shrugged. "My mom wasn't too keen on getting married either. She's the cautious type, wanted to wait a couple of years to see if they lasted. But they were needled to death by family members on both sides to make it official before my older sister came into the world."

Antonio was glad they lived in a different time from when couples married just because a baby was on the way. "Are your parents still together?"

"They are! They have a good marriage at least from what I can see."

"So just the one sibling for you too?"

"Yep." Julia chuckled, she was close to her sister even though they lived in different states.

"It seems we're both part of small families." Antonio rubbed a finger along her hand. "See, we already have something in common, I'm hoping we have much more before the night is over."

"We'll see." Julia slid her hand away, as their main course was being delivered.

They had barely gotten into the meal when the live band started, and having a conversation became nearly impossible. However, Julia was content, settling in to enjoy the wonderful music and excellent food. She tried keeping the talking to a minimum because it meant Antonio had to lean in close.

The man had already by chance, or on purpose, grazed her ear with his mouth several times. And she'd swear the tip of his tongue touched her at least once. That plus the husky scent of his cologne left her feeling off kilter. Not to mention she wasn't into screaming over the noise in the first place. By the time the set was over it was pretty much time to leave.

\* \* \*

Antonio had done that thing again where he took every opportunity to touch her. Guiding her with a hand low on her back as they walked to the car, brushing his shoulder against her own. And each contact sent a little sizzle of awareness through her.

The drive back to her house had that slightly uncomfortable feeling one might get in the waiting room of a small gynecologist office. Sure everyone in the waiting room was a woman too, but no one really tries to make conversation. *That's* what the car felt like now.

Thankfully, it took less than thirty minutes to reach her place in Melvindale and she had never been so glad to be home. Julia would have hopped out of the car but he was too quick, coming around to open the door before she unbuckled the seatbelt. Doing the hand thing again as they walked up her drive, taking the liberty of going even lower this time, resting it on the swell of her ass trying to be slick. Julia just picked up her pace and pointedly blocked the door with her back as she turned to him.

"Thanks Antonio for tonight. Dinner was really good and so was the music."

"You're welcome. I'm glad you let me take you out."

"Yes...about that. We-"

Julia didn't get anything else out because his tongue was in her mouth. He'd caught her completely off guard, grabbing her face with both hands. They both tasted like wine, but she had a feeling she could get drunk off of him better than any alcohol. He didn't touch her anywhere else, at least not with his hands. But he crushed his body against hers, and she could feel his peaking arousal. Julia kept her hands pressed against the door, *she* didn't want to risk touching him, her body already felt like a live wire from a simple kiss. When he finally pulled back, her eyes fluttered open, and damn the man for having the nerve to lick his lips.

"I'd love to come in."

"Umm no, that won't be happening. Look I don't think we're a good idea...romantically." He took a step back and thankfully her legs held. "I'm not the kind of girl for you. I'm not a "Jenny from the block" type and I think you're looking for something I'm not."

"I mean you definitely have something in common with J.Lo." Antonio gazed at her ass. "Why don't you let me in so I can get a better look."

"I told you at the start this wouldn't work, but now you can't say I didn't try. Tonight was cool but anything sexual is out."

"Maybe I can at least call you from time to time." He persisted.

"Maybe you shouldn't...goodnight Antonio."

# Chapter Three

Julia spent the rest of the weekend trying to get that kiss out of her mind. It had been just how she expected it to be, because yeah she'd had a few fantasies about it since meeting him. Intense and overwhelming is the only way to describe it. She hadn't been expecting him to just *take* the kiss like that. True it irritated her when a man asked, always had, but normally a man would make eye contact then lean in slowly, allowing a woman to see it coming and act accordingly. Antonio had been bold while she'd acted like a rabbit, stuck to one spot like an idiot.

Her traitorous body had responded to his act of taking, the way his tongue invaded her mouth had excited her, just like the shameless way he'd pressed his hips into hers made Julia want more. This was why she had to stay away from the man, she couldn't risk getting hooked on great sex. Besides, he wasn't serious about anything more than getting in her pants.

He'd flashed his car, a fancy restaurant and expected that to be enough to get her into bed. Julia was sure for many women it would be enough, which was their prerogative. She wasn't judging, in her younger days that might have worked on her too. If a girl was just looking for fun and a nice workout between the sheets, Antonio would fit the bill. Fun wasn't the top priority on her list right now, in fact she wasn't *looking* for anything.

Her last relationship had disappointed her to the point she was giving up for the moment. It hadn't even been his fault or hers, it just didn't work. Even so, she was tired of being hurt by failed relationships. Right now she didn't want the distraction of good sex with nothing else, nor was she looking for Mr. Right. Julia just wanted some peace. Maybe the right person hadn't been placed in her life yet because she had some work to do on herself?

Hell, she didn't know, but she did know getting tangled up with Antonio would be messy for her, their friend group and now the center. Julia just had to ignore her body that screamed it would be *so worth it!* She'd stayed true to her word and given him one date, now she could go back to pretending he didn't exist. If need be Kimberly could work the mentoring schedule so they spent as little time together as possible. But Julia hoped Antonio had gotten the message loud and clear and would leave her alone.

*  *  *

Antonio knew he should probably let the whole thing with Julia be—he also knew he wasn't going to. Some of this was his ego talking, as he had never been so distinctly dismissed after a date. But he also knew damn well she wanted him, had felt it in his bones after that kiss. He felt strongly there was more potential than just being "friends" between them.

When Wednesday hit he decided to give her a call anyway. Dinner had reconfirmed there was a spark between them, one he had no desire to deny, even if she obviously did. Why she didn't want to explore it was a mystery he was determined to unravel. He knew she was single, wasn't dating anyone else, as he'd asked outright.

Something he didn't actually do that often, as it wasn't his concern if a woman was stepping out on her old man since he wasn't looking for anything serious. Plus women usually asked him first and the topic was broached that way. He had the feeling Julia would never date two guys, so at least that wasn't a reason why she was so resistant to him.

As far as he knew he hadn't wronged some friend of hers, and Antonio knew Robert would never gossip about his personal life. Which left him unable to figure out why Julia had such a horrible impression of him. Antonio wasn't a saint but he wasn't a monster either. He dated here and there, probably no more than any other man his age. Frankly probably a bit less.

His job was demanding, any spare time outside of that was spent relaxing. But when the itch hit him he scratched it, usually with party girls who were looking for a good time. They wanted a man with enough money to take them to fancy places, get them in the best clubs and break them off in a crib of his own. He provided all that, and they provided entertainment and a warm willing body. No harm no foul.

The way Julia seemed determined to avoid him you would think he had a "freak of the week" or something, when the truth was he averaged two dates a month if he was lucky. Anyway, he had a feeling if he pushed a little he could get past the weird wall Julia reserved just for him. A classy, smart and sexy woman like her deserved to be taken out and shown a good time. She needed more downtime in her life, so she could be as relaxed as she had been on that island.

Antonio wanted to see that again, maybe even be the one responsible for it. She seemed pent up and he wasn't really talking in a sexual way, though that was possible too. It hadn't escaped him that she hadn't touched him during their kiss. Thinking about it now had him shifting on the couch, so he finally stopped stalling and pulled up her number, blocking the caller ID before calling. He was fully aware she had it in her to ignore his calls—that's if his number wasn't already blocked.

"Hello."

"Hey, it's Antonio."

A few seconds of silence before a weary sigh came over the line. "I thought I told you not to call."

"You did and I heard you, but I didn't like the way things ended."

"I wasn't aware you had to like my wishes to abide by them."

"True. Look you don't owe me an explanation but I sure would appreciate one. Help me understand."

"I'm sorry, what exactly don't you understand and what would you like an explanation to?" Julia asked, confused.

"I thought we had a nice night together. You enjoyed the food, the music..."

"I did, remember I thanked you for all that."

"Okay, so why don't you want to go out, or even talk to me. Where did the night go wrong? And don't tell me it was the hot as fuck kiss we shared either. Because I know damn well it felt as good to you, as it did to me."

Oh! If he wanted brutal honesty, she could give that to him.

"You want to know where it went wrong? I'll be happy to tell you. From the moment you picked me up in your flashy car. Then it continued with you taking us to an expensive place where we only had about twenty-five minutes of real conversation before the music started. You didn't *really* want to get to know me. You wanted to impress me, thinking that would be enough to make my panties come off for you.

Well here's a newsflash, while everything was nice I wasn't impressed. It definitely didn't rate high enough for me to invite you into my house! I'm not into all that highbrow stuff, and I *definitely* hate it when a man thinks I'm needy or greedy enough to be swayed by a nice meal and a fancy car. Does that clarify things for you now Mr. Alvarez?"

"Yeah...it does." Well damn. "Okay, you caught me, I *was* trying to impress you, which I see failed miserably. But believe it or not, I'd rather hear that than the B.S. answers you normally give me. I admit I'm attracted to you and I took my shot at your house. I fucked up the time we should've been using to get to know each other. Let me make it up to you, go out with me this weekend."

"Are you crazy?" Julia let out an incredulous laugh, this man just didn't give up.

"I've been called many things in my life but crazy isn't one of them. I'm serious, let me try again to give you a fun time. We'll do something lowkey, someplace we can talk if you want, or relax if you prefer. Give me another chance."

"What makes you think you deserve another one? Sometimes one strike is all you get Antonio."

He chuckled, she hadn't outright told him no, so there was still hope.

"That kiss makes me think you should give *us* another try, not that anything has to progress in that area...yet. I'm asking you to allow me one more date, no other strings attached. I'll keep my lips to myself the entire evening, I promise on the kids."

"That's a shitty thing to promise on."

"No, it's just how serious I am. I'm a man of my word and I just gave it to *you*. Let me take you out this Saturday."

While she didn't really know his level of integrity, she knew the men he rolled with. Though why she was giving his offer *any* consideration was an enigma? What she needed to do was tell him to kick rocks, but said this instead.

"The 4th of July is this Saturday, Antonio."

"And? That's even better, there will be tons of stuff going on that we can do. Just say yes. I get it, you apparently don't like giving three strikes—but damn—give a man at least two! Don't forget you didn't hate our date at the end of the day."

There was a long pause before Julia said, "I'll meet you wherever we go."

"No problem." He readily agreed.

"Make it some kind of activity. If you don't plan to have a meaningful conversation with me, the least you can do is keep me entertained."

"I'm hoping to do both, but I hear you. Anything else?"

"Just don't make me regret this. Let me know the details by early Friday at the latest."

"Yes ma'am." Antonio didn't mind her bossy tone. "You won't regret it, I promise."

# Chapter Four

Julia pulled her sensible and fully paid-off car into the Clawson Festival grounds on what was unquestionably a perfect 4th of July day. She'd had an early dinner at her parents, enjoying time with extended family for a mid-day cookout. Now at six, she was parking next to Antonio's car, in the back reaches of the field being used as a parking lot. Waving, as she lifted her sunglasses to appraise him.

He had on tan cargo shorts with a peach polo shirt, his own shades hooked on his collar, with that winning smile of his pointed her way. The sight of him tightened her stomach, why did the man have to look so darn good no matter what? Snapping out of it, Julia ran a hand down her checkered blue, green and white sundress before walking forward.

It was 82 degrees and sunny, she wasn't going to burn to death because of him. Her spaghetti strap dress was low cut, though not enough to be indecent, while the bottom bellowed out and fell a few inches above her knees. If he couldn't control himself over a normal summer outfit then that was his problem. She did have a light sweater in the car just in case it got really cool later on or the bugs came out in force. But that was a worry for another time, the first part of her day had been great and she was going to make the best of the second half too.

"You made it!"

"Of course I did, I said I would come."

"I know what you *said* Julia, but I can't get a good read on you yet."

"Good to know." She said unapologetically as they started to walk. "Why are we parked so far back?"

"Walking is good for you, plus I wanted to make sure you had a spot by me and it was fuller upfront."

"Walking *is* good. But hiking is another thing." She quipped. "I confess when you sent me the details I was surprised. Didn't take you for the type to like this kind of stuff."

"What's not to like? Who doesn't like fairs?" Antonio questioned. "I mean you have rides, food and they'll be fireworks tonight. A person has to be a serial killer not to like fireworks."

Julia laughed. "I think even killers like them. Anyway, this is cool even if it was a bit of a drive. So many cities never do fireworks on the actual holiday, so I'm excited."

"Agreed, so what do you want to do first?"

"I'm actually really looking forward to browsing the arts and crafts booths, but let's hit the rides before that."

"Sounds like a solid plan to me. Pick your poison."

Julia went over to the 110ft. free-fall ride to start their evening off. Standing in line Antonio looked at her skeptically, "Are you sure about this?"

"I am. I've always wanted to try one. And this is just tall enough for my taste. Don't tell me a macho man like you is scared."

"I like to think all smart men would be apprehensive about free falling ten stories."

"What if I said I'll hold your hand." Julia batted her eyes at him. "Would that help?"

"It's a whole different story if I have incentives. Let's hope this deathtrap doesn't break while we're on it."

It was almost ten minutes before they were seated and the compartment slowly made it to the top. But when Antonio tried to grab her hand, she pulled away.

"I thought you said you'd hold my hand?"

Julia grinned. "I lied."

"That's so—*messed uupppp!*"

The drop had him screaming and her laughing. In fact, Julia was still laughing when they got off.

"I'm glad this isn't a theme park where they take pictures." Antonio gave her the evil-eye.

"And I *sooo* wish it was. I'd gladly pay for a picture of you hollering."

"Whatever." Antonio tried to play it off. "I was just caught off guard is all. I stopped after a few seconds."

"The entire thing was only *a few seconds*." Deciding to stop teasing him she steered them over to another ride. "Let's do the SkyFall thing next."

Antonio looked at the next gravity-defying ride she wanted him to go on. It was a big metal X with four gondolas on the end that swung back and forth until you were straight up in the air, upside down.

"Why are you trying to kill me? Whatever, I have great life insurance, my mother will have that at least."

They rode it, and this time Julia was the one doing all the screaming and clutching at his arm. All while squeezing her knees tight so her dress didn't fly up, exposing her lady bits. He appreciated her diligence as he wanted to be the only one here to see that. Antonio was shocked by how relaxed and open she seemed today. Maybe it was the holiday, or the rides, whatever it was he would take it. He was an easy-going man so he appreciated environments that played to that *and* the company of others who made him feel the same.

This was the Julia he'd seen at the wedding. Next to all the other women in the group, she could come off as the quiet one. But it had been crystal clear she knew how to have fun with people who made her comfortable. Antonio was glad she was starting to feel at ease with him. Next, it was his turn to choose and he picked the Gravitron since he'd loved it as a kid.

She didn't have to worry about her dress as they were getting plastered to the wall by 4G's. They decided to take a break after that and he bought her some cotton candy and snagged himself a hotdog. When he thought she wasn't looking he bit a mouthful of her sugary confection only to be poked in the shoulder. But she showed him an unexpected gesture of generosity by pulling him off a big chunk. Thanking her, he made a show of licking it off his fingers only for Julia's eyes to narrow, but he saw the color creeping into her cheeks as well. She wasn't immune to him and they both knew it.

This local celebration in the small town of Clawson was a mesh-up of a county fair and a carnival. They had a 3-legged race, a water balloon toss and other folksy events going on along with the rides, all of which seemed to please his date.

"Oooh, let's do the 3-legged race!"

"Why are you trying to fall in public? If you tip over your dress won't leave much to the imagination." Antonio pointed out. "Be assured I'm not complaining...just stating a fact."

"Damn, you're right." Julia twisted her lips with annoyance. "I want to sign up for one of these events though."

"How about the water balloon toss? Worse that can happen is you get a little wet. Then all the men get a treat."

"Stop it, this is a family event." But she giggled a little. "Fine, let's do it. I have a sweater in my car, plus it's so hot I'll dry quickly. *You* just better not try to get me wet on purpose."

"I promise." Antonio sent her a serious look only to have her burst out laughing.

"I can see your fingers crossed idiot."

"Well then, don't say I didn't warn you."

They signed up but had to wait for the next round, so they stood around watching. Somebody had thought it would be a great idea to make this game even harder than normal. There were lanes of orange cones set up for each pair, and five teams went at once. The goal was to make it down the lanes of cones, tossing the balloon as the game master called out instructions. The first person to get to the end with their balloon intact won. When their turn arrived Antonio had her pick the water balloon.

"I don't want to hear any complaints that it wasn't a good size for your little hands."

"My hands aren't that small." But she studied the selection before picking one. "You just make sure your aim and throwing arm is on point today."

When the game master called out the first "toss!" they started walking. It was a struggle to stay behind their cones, look at where the other person was, and time their throws all at once. Julia loved it, and couldn't stop laughing at the absurdity of it all. Clearly, it brought out Antonio's competitive drive as he yelled at her to pay attention and speed up, even though they were already tripping trying to go so fast. Right now, they were neck and neck with a team made up of teenagers.

"Come on Julia, a little faster!"

They were about 10 feet from the finish line when the next toss she sent him was too forceful and slipped out of his fingers before bursting on his legs.

"Oh no!" Julia screamed at the same time the announcer said they had a winner. Rushing over to Antonio she covered her mouth. "I'm so sorry."

"Are you really? Because I hear some snickering."

"True, but I'm still sorry. At least you don't have on full-length pants." She grabbed his arm dragging them towards the food vendors. "Come on, let's dry you off."

# Chapter Five

Antonio was about to tell her it wasn't a big deal until she grabbed a wad of napkins and dropped down on her heels to dry off his legs. *Shitttt*, he may not have won the game, but seeing her at his feet, hands rubbing along his legs was a good enough reward for him! Didn't even matter that she was doing a brisk, efficient rubdown either. He just knew the visual of her like this would be in his head tonight.

"Okay, that's enough, stop before you rub off my skin."

"I think I got most of it anyway. Sorry again. What do you say we leave the games and finally look at the booths."

"I think that sounds like a *safe* thing to do."

A good sixty vendors were broken into about ten rows, and Julia was determined to do it the most methodical way. So they started from the row furthest out and worked their way in. She was a sucker for handmade or unique things and it wasn't long before she was breaking out her card. Buying a hand-painted purse for herself, then deciding to get one for all the centers' co-founders as gifts. A present and apology for how rigid she was with money.

It was a hazard of her occupation, and good business sense to be thrifty. Julia wasn't overly frugal with her own money, but the center ran on what the four women put in every month and occasional donations. All to cover supplies, food, utilities and outings that weren't free. Their center was quite large, the thought being for the future when they might expand into a variety of programs. A good thing too, since they'd just added the boys. Camden, Robert and Thomas had insisted on putting a grand into the "upkeep" pot each year once they found out about it.

It was her job to make sure their money lasted and was allocated where it was needed, and not wasted where it wasn't. That meant she often had to be Ebenezer Scrooge. Luckily, Kimberly was working on their first grant proposal, so fingers crossed they'd start getting funding from the outside. Anyway, she was hoping to surprise them with the gift and she'd probably stuff other little knick-knacks in it too. At another table, she found a small painting for her living room and a few small figurines. It was here that Antonio bought his first purchase.

"Those are so cute! Are you getting them for yourself or as a gift?"

"Why would I buy myself an angel figurine?"

"Just because you're a man doesn't mean you can't like something delicate like that. I bet your actual guardian Angel has to work overtime keeping *you* out of trouble."

"You're probably right, especially as a teenager." Antonio laughed, giving her a cheeky grin. "I don't have a problem *owning* one as a man, I have two that my mother gave me. She's like you, thinks I need a little extra protection. These are for her, she collects them. I had to buy her a curio a few years ago just to store them all. At the places I shop it's rare that I come across them, so I thought I'd snag a few."

"That's sweet." The vendor who had been shamelessly listening commented. "I'll give you the two for forty instead of fifty."

"Thank you, but that's okay. You're the one doing me a favor, my mom will love these, and I'll get extra points in the favorite son department." Antonio handed over the cash and started walking away when the lady called out.

"Hey, you gave me too much!" She was holding three twenty's in her hand.

"Keep it, your art is worth it."

"Thanks!" The vendor turned to Julia. "And honey, keep that one. He's a good catch!"

"You hear that Julia, someone thinks I'm a good catch."

"That's because she doesn't know you *and* you paid her extra."

He looked down at her, pulling her a little closer with the arm he had slung around her shoulders "Neither do you."

"I'm starting to...and maybe you're not so horrible." Julia broke eye contact but ended up looking at his lips which was even worse, so she kept talking to distract them both.

"That was nice of you. I have a second cousin who makes carvings and it's a lot of hard work and passion. It's one of the reasons I love supporting local artists. Their stuff seems high because we're used to mass production prices, but folks deserve to make money for their effort."

"I agree, I never have a problem paying for anything custom-made. There's also no price on making my mother happy."

"Are you a mama's boy?" Julia needled.

"Do you know many Hispanic men who aren't? But no, not if you mean is my mother all up in my business or runs my life because she's not. I lucked out and got the coolest mother there is. She's always let me be my own person. However, she is the number one lady in my life, so yeah I try to spoil her here and there."

"Mothers definitely deserve it. Now I feel the need to find mine a gift. Let's check out these other rows and see what they have."

They went down each lane, stopping at any tent that caught one of their interest. There was no real rush as the fireworks were still a ways off, though they did barely get done looking before the vendors shut down at 9:30. After that they walked around a bit, eating junk food they didn't need while crowd-watching. Around 9:40 Julia told him she wanted to go on one more ride.

"The Ferris wheel? When I asked you about it before you said you didn't want to go."

"I know and I didn't want to go *then*, I want to go now. I was waiting until it was darker, I like when the ride lights up and the stars are just peeking out, it's better that way."

"You realize it's a full ten-minute ride once it starts, right? We might miss the fireworks." He warned.

"We won't, I've timed it. We'll be off before they even start."

"If you say so." Antonio mumbled, not convinced.

Watching as she put the smaller bags into the larger ones, so when they boarded five minutes later they only had two bags to worry about. Each put one on their side before sitting hip to hip.

"These things are so slow, I've never liked them." He complained.

"That's because you need something to be racing around all the time. It's a peaceful ride, now be quiet so I can enjoy it."

"Whatever you say."

Antonio shut his mouth, stretching his arm along the back of the seat, pulling her in closer as it rocked and rose while more people got on. Two minutes later they finally picked up speed as the ride officially started. From up here the lights from the various rides lit up the night.

As they went around and round she relaxed even more, eventually laying her head on his shoulder. So close that he could smell her hair, some type of herbal shampoo that smelled like flowers. He liked it, then again he liked a lot of things about her. She was sweet, but not a pushover by far. Antonio didn't feel like he always had to be "on" with her, she was comfortable.

Not a diva like a lot of the women he usually took out, it was like she didn't realize how hot she actually was.

Like today, her outfit was cute, sexy and fresh. Her shoulder-length hair was pinned up on both sides to stay out of her face, though she'd made no attempt to curl it which made sense with the humidity. Everything about her was sensible, down to the low heeled sandals she wore. It was no wonder she was wary of him, Antonio would agree he wasn't the "sensible" choice.

He wasn't a solid bet unless a woman was clearly looking for a good time. Much more than that he couldn't really say. He wasn't actively against relationships, just hadn't felt the need to enter one in over five years. Shorter entanglements seemed to work best for his current lifestyle. Antonio supposed if he ever found someone that made him want to settle down he'd be all for it.

Was Julia the one? He wasn't ready to say all that, but did feel drawn to her. Enjoyed being around her, even when she was giving him a hard time. Was some of what drew him to her the challenge aspect...probably. He had no problem pulling women when he wanted to, which was why her being so firmly opposed to him was a provocation to his mind. But today had been a lot of fun and he'd only thought about sleeping with her once.

Admittedly it was tricky deciding if it was worth dealing with people in an inner friend circle, as he firmly believed in not shitting where you ate. But sitting with her pressed against his side felt right, especially when she was looking at him with those big, tawny eyes he could fall into.

"See, told you this would be nice. It's so peaceful and pretty up here."

"Yeah, it's pretty alright."

Antonio brushed away a stray hair from her forehead and they both knew his comment wasn't about the stars or lights. He saw her eyes widen with awareness and he shifted to focus on her lips. Right now he damned himself for his promise, because he wanted to kiss her so fucking bad. Looking away he stroked her bare shoulder instead, trying to be content with that.

Until that charged moment Julia had dreaded the ride ending, but now it felt like it was taking forever to finish. Being snuggled up with Antonio felt cozy, and the look he'd given her a moment ago made her think she was about to be kissed. Surprisingly she wanted him to. Exiting the ride disappointment set in, though Julia knew "no kissing" was probably for the best.

"Umm, do you want to go find a place to watch the fireworks? We have five minutes or so?"

"Let's head to the car and put our stuff up first." Antonio suggested. "I have a couple of pop-up chairs in my trunk, I see a lot of folks setting up over on that lawn area."

It took them at least four minutes to make it back to their cars, and after separating their packages and storing them in their own vehicles she just shook her head as he went to pull the chairs out the trunk.

"We might as well just watch from here, they're about to start."

"Sounds good to me, hop on in."

*

She got comfortable in his swanky ride as he rolled down the windows as the first burst of color filled the sky. They watched in silence, both captivated for a full five minutes. But even fireworks couldn't distract her from the man sitting beside her. She chanced a glance his way, only to find him looking straight in her direction.

Julia pointed at the window. "The fireworks are out there."

"I know...I'm more mesmerized at what's in the car."

"I thought you liked fireworks." Julia said softly, pulse jumping at the look of desire he was giving her.

"I do, I just wish we were making some of our own."

"Then why aren't you?" Why had she said that and why was she holding her breath to see if he would make a move—he didn't.

"I'm a man of my word Julia, so I better turn around and watch the sky."

He did just that while she tried to remember what he was talking about, then his promise not to kiss her came to mind. She knew he was doing the right thing, so why did she lean over the divide, giving him a light kiss on the cheek.

"That's for today, it's been great. Thank you." Julia whispered in his ear.

Antonio didn't speak but turned his head until their lips were only a hair apart, before literally hauling her over, so she was straddling his lap. It happened so quickly she didn't have time to say anything. Julia would have been surprised by his strength, but for the fact she'd seen him without a shirt before and knew he had plenty of compact muscles. As she tried to sit up, she failed. Like many men he had his seat tilted back, plus his arm across her lower back kept her pressed against his chest.

"I thought you were supposed to be behaving." Why was she breathlessly uttering nonsense instead of telling him to let her go?

"I said I'd keep my lips to myself." He gripped the back of her thighs and dragged his hands up to palm her ass, squeezing.

*Jesus*, she had on a thong! "I never said anything about my hands."

She opened her mouth only to have him flick out his tongue to run it across her bottom lip.

"*Antonio*...people will see." She moaned instead of telling him to stop.

"Everyone is watching the sky." But he took one hand away from her skin to roll up the tinted windows, enclosing them in. "If you want me, you should kiss me."

Maybe there was holiday magic in the air because Julia didn't hesitate to press her lips against his. Like that—the genie was out of the bottle and passion flowed through their blood! Antonio brought a hand from her heavenly backside to the nape of her neck, slanting his mouth to sweeten the kiss. He tasted a hint of cotton candy or was it just the essence of her? He didn't know and didn't care, but he liked it and wanted more.

He couldn't believe he had his hands on her at last, and that she was enthusiastically melting against him. With the hand still under her dress, he ran a finger between her butt cheeks, then over the thin scrap of material covering her pussy. The shock made her cry out and she pulled her mouth from his. They locked eyes as he still stroked, letting hers get hazy before he demanded, "Kiss me again cariño."

She did, and he continued to stoke the fire inside her. Until she squirmed, kissing his jaw and neck, her hands under his polo grabbing at his taut stomach. So he shouldn't have been surprised at the sting of her nails when at last he pulled her panties aside, slipping two fingers inside her warmth. He fingered her fast and hard, and her control snapped as she started fucking his hand in return. Minutes later she was shaking from a mini-climax, recovering only to claw at his belt, tearing at his zipper. Antonio loved every second of it!

While she was trying to get in his pants he scooped her breasts from the halter top of the dress with his free hand. Caressing them as she finally freed him from his shorts, shivering as she wrapped a soft hand around his shaft. Damn, she was killing him already. To stop himself from saying anything that could break the spell, he eagerly sucked a nipple into his wet mouth.

He needn't have worried about slowing down, because Julia seemed to be speeding up, lifting off his now slick fingers before guiding his dick to her entrance. Antonio couldn't believe it, but his body sure pushed up as she bore down. Her warmth surrounding him like a heated fist. The roof of his car was semi-low, so she was bent forward enough for him to grab her mouth in another searing kiss. This time he took and devoured, even as he let her steer their sexual ride.

Antonio wasn't sure how long he enjoyed the high of being fucked, before using what brainpower he had left to lay the seat as flat as possible. Then he was able to lock her against his chest, while his feet found purchase on whatever was in reach so he could fuck her back. Thrusting up into her folds he tried to catch her cries of pleasure with his mouth, not that either of them gave a shit by that time.

The music and the fireworks drowned them out anyway, the lights and sounds adding to the beat their bodies made. Antonio watched her face through half-closed eyes. The sounds coming from her swollen lips, the blush of arousal in her cheeks, all increased the pleasure he felt. They both became more frantic as the fireworks marched towards their crescendo, right along with their climax. Julia exploded first, clenching around him, squeezing so tight that his remaining thrusts lost tempo. When it was his turn he saw colored stars behind his eyes—bigger and brighter than anything outside.

# Chapter Six

Julia tried not to think about the amazing sex with Antonio last weekend, which was a tremendously hard thing to do. Every time she closed her eyes for a stress break at work, or at bedtime it replayed in her head. She couldn't believe how hot he'd gotten her so quickly, making her mindless and shameless with need. Even as a teenager she'd never had sex in a car, much less in a public place with people around. People's families were there for god's sake!

It didn't matter that she tried to make herself feel better with the fact it had been dark, in the very back of a huge parking field. None of that stopped her from thinking she'd lost her mind. The two had laid there for a full minute after both their bodies had popped like the final fireworks. Sounds of the crowd coming to their vehicles had pushed her to slip her dress back up and ease off his lap. Clumsily getting back into her own seat, as he'd righted his.

After inanely thanking him for "a great day" and muttering an excuse that she needed to go before the crowd reached them. Julia had hopped in her car without letting him get a word out, driving home with shaky legs and a still throbbing coño. Now days later her mind was saying "never again" while her kitty was saying "sign me up for the next round!"

She had hoped he would disappear, having gotten what he was after. That way Julia wouldn't have to worry if her body won over her brains. Sadly her wish didn't come true because Antonio texted her the next day *and* the next. He hadn't said anything boasting or even sexual, just asking how she was and letting her know he had enjoyed their time together too. Still, she had ignored them all.

But when she got a text on Tuesday wishing her a good week, she finally broke down and responded. Saying it wasn't him, that she just wasn't interested in taking their night together any further. He'd asked "why" and she'd said her decision was final, so the why of it didn't matter. After that crickets, and Julia had been relieved Antonio had finally taken the hint. Or so she had thought before coming back from lunch on Wednesday to find a long ribbon-tied box on her desk.

"Hey, Candace did you see who put this here?"

"Yeah, reception brought it in." Peeking over the cubicle Candace grinned. "We've all been taking bets on if these are from your folks or some guy you're dating. Tim of little faith keeps doubling down that they're from your folks. But I don't know, something about the packaging has me thinking it's personal."

Glancing at Tim who was also standing, Julia shook her head.

"I'm disappointed that you don't think a guy would send me flowers Tim."

"I didn't say that, just that it was more probable they came from your parents. They've been known to send you some from time to time. Unless you've gotten back together with Jordan..." Tim let that hang in the air as everyone seemed to hold their collective breaths to see if it was true.

"No I'm not back with Jordan, plus he would know I wouldn't like getting these at work."

"You are so strange to me." Jennifer, another coworker commented. "I would *love* to get flowers at work."

"Well, that's why you're you and I'm me. I like keeping my personal life just that, personal."

Jennifer was an attention whore and everyone knew it.

"Okay, whatever." Candace waived away their bickering. "Since these *did* come to your job why don't you open them. I almost peeked, but I didn't! Knew you would take my head off if I did. Plus the way they're wrapped I couldn't get in without it being obvious."

"You should be commended on your restraint." Julia said dryly.

Turning she slid off the ribbon before setting the top aside, only to dig through a mound of tissue paper before finding the most perfect long-stemmed yellow roses she had ever seen. A half a dozen to be exact.

"Oooohhh" Candace squealed. "So pretty!"

They were beautiful! Wondering if they were in fact from Jordan, she flipped open the card, truly surprised to see Antonio's name.

**I had a great time last weekend
and think this could be the start of a beautiful friendship
Call me—Antonio**

After a few seconds of gawking at the note, Julia picked up the roses and gently took one from the batch. Turning she handed it over to Candace, then another to Jennifer and Carla who were nearby. Taking the other three she passed them out to the other women around the office. Margerie, Catherine and took the last to her boss Susan. When she came back Tim was standing with his hands on his hips.

"Just want you to know I find it sexist you only shared with the women. Dave and I have feelings too."

Julia grinned, knowing he was pulling her chain.

"Sorry guys, I only had six. I'll get you next time I get flowers out the blue."

"Yeah, whatever. Tell me was I right, were they from your parents?"

"Yep." Julia lied. "They just sent them as a general pick me up. Told me to have a great rest of the week. That's why I figured I'd spread the joy."

That seemed to settle everyone down so she could send off a text.

> **Julia:** I got the flowers, they were very nice but I wish you hadn't sent them
>
> **Tone:** Why? Do you not like yellow?
>
> **Julia:** The flowers I liked, just not you

There was a full minute pause before she got a reply to that.

> **Tone:** I think we both know that's not true. Did I do something wrong?
>
> **Julia:** No...you didn't. Just don't send flowers to my job again
>
> **Julia:** I'd prefer it if you didn't text me again either

Another long break before a final text came.

> **Tone:** Okay

Julia didn't realize she'd been holding her breath until she let it out. Maybe this time he'd take the message to heart and that was a good thing, right? Her stomach was only tied up in knots because of lunch, it had zero to do with him, was the lie Julia told herself.

* * *

Friday was here and she like a few billion other folks around the world, had survived the workweek. The weekend was a few hours away, then she could relax. So at three o'clock

Julia had her head down, focused on work when commotion at their suite door made her look up.

A guy who she thought worked on the second floor was ushering in Antonio, before giving him a pat on the back and walking away. Spotting her he casually made his way to her desk with a big bouquet of flowers in his hands as Julia heard the squeak of chairs swiveling around. Damn all these nosy ass people! For her part, she stayed where she was, her back ramrod straight until he finally stopped.

"Hey, Julia."

"What are you doing here." She hissed.

"You said not to send you flowers, so I brought them. I would have let you know I was coming but you told me not to text either." He gave her a Cheshire cat grin at using her own words against her.

Popping up and grabbing him by the elbow, she propelled them to the door. "Let's have this conversation out in the hall shall we."

Julia didn't miss the women openly ogling him either in his three-piece suit. Several even had the nerve to give her a wink as she almost shoved him out the door. At that moment she wished they didn't have a stupid glass entrance, as everyone could clearly see them through it.

"Have you lost your damn mind coming to my job? How did you even get up here?" Even though her voice was low, anyone looking would know her body language eluded to a heated conversation.

"I know a lot of people, a buddy works here. You left me no choice. I wanted to know why you basically ghosted me. It can't be that I sucked in the sack, because we both know that would be a damn lie."

"Keep your voice down." Julia brushed her hair away in agitation. "Look you know it wasn't that. I just don't think it's something to be repeated and I didn't think *you'd* want to anyway. You got what you wanted, to bang the "pent-up" accountant and I got what I needed, let's not pretend we have something more."

"We don't know what we have one way or the other with you acting like a scared cat. You didn't even have the nerve to tell me this."

"I told you, you just didn't want to hear it. I'm sure you're more used to being the ghostee but I didn't ghost you. You were just hard-headed and refused to take no for an answer."

"You might have a point, but I wasn't just out to sleep with you. I've said from the start I wanted us to get to know each other. We get along fine when you aren't purposely starting shit with me. We now know the attraction we've been feeling translates *extremely well* in the sex department. So yeah, excuse the hell out of me if I don't want to throw that away. Maybe that's what you're used to from other men, but I'm not them. I want to see you again."

"I don't know what to say...but once was enough for me."

Antonio smiled and leaned in close. "It's you who keeps making this about sex only. Also, you came twice...I'm the one who only came once. I think you owe me for that and I'm not talking sex per se, but give me another date."

"Didn't you already talk me into a second date?" Julia's eyes narrowed "Isn't that what got us here in the first place?"

"I don't see anything wrong with what happened. And I'm confused by the fact that you do. I'm giving you a chance to prove *I* wasn't used for sex."

"You are absurd and pushy." Julia spat out.

"And you're stubborn and unreasonable, but I still like you. Plus, I got you red flowers this time." He joked, pushing them into her arms. "I figured maybe you really don't like yellow."

"There was nothing wrong with the first roses, they were just as beautiful as these. One more date, and If I tell you to leave me alone after this and you don't, I'm blocking your number and alerting building security."

"Fine, I agree. Since you like low-key, why don't we Netflix and chill? Tomorrow at your place, on your own turf."

"Sure whatever. Get out of here before all my co-workers break an ankle walking past the damn door just to look at us."

# Chapter Seven

Julia had gone back in with a fake smile, stopping at Dave and Tim's desk to plunk down a rose.

"Told you I'd get you next time."

"You also told us those other flowers were from your parents." Tim recalled.

"They were!" Julia lied easily. "Why do you have so little faith in me Tim? Can't a woman get flowers from her parents and a friend in the same week?"

She wasn't sure if the guys bought it, but the ladies in her office sure didn't. Giving her sly looks and declining the gorgeous flowers, which was how she ended up taking the rest home. The home that Antonio would be sitting in tomorrow. Lord, why hadn't she just cussed the man out so things could go back to normal.

She just had to remember that she didn't have to give in to whatever he wanted over what she did. Only problem was it was getting harder to figure out exactly what he wanted, much less herself. Spending an evening with him in her home wouldn't be that bad...right...maybe? When he arrived at her place at six-thirty Julia got out of her head and opened the door.

"Hey!"

"Come on in Antonio. Why do you sound so surprised to see me, we had a date."

"Because honestly, I was expecting you not to answer. Or a family of four would open the door and tell me you'd sold this house to them at a steal just the night before."

"You're an idiot." She laughed, closing and locking the door behind him. "What do you have there? You didn't have to bring anything."

"Sure I did. How can it be a date if there's no food?"

"I thought this was Netflix and chill? Like a quasi-apology for me semi trying to ghost you." Julia rubbed her hands against her pants. "If I'd known I would have thrown something together..."

"I would never put you out like that last minute. Relax, I took care of it. Well, assuming you like Lasagna?"

"Who doesn't?" Her smile was back. "I like it a lot actually."

"Excellent. Should I set this up in the kitchen or..."

"Umm no, I'll grab some plates and we can eat in front of the TV. I was looking forward to zoning out on some shows, my plan before our little get together came up. What would you like to drink? I don't keep hard liquor in the house, but have wine, water, and juice."

"Water is good for now."

"Okay."

They headed off in separate directions and she shook her head in irritation. Why the heck had she implied she would cook him dinner. She would not have, he was a grown man who could feed himself and apparently he had. Getting what she needed from the kitchen Julia came back to see him with the remote in hand, already flipping through movies.

"Is it a genetic thing that men have to attach themselves to a remote if they're within 50ft. of one?"

"Sorry," he said sheepishly. "You did say you had something in mind. What's your flavor for tonight?"

Julia sat, folding her legs beneath her. "Go to my queue, I just added season two of "You" yesterday so it should be up there."

*

They ate while laughing at the crazy storyline of the show, though she did compare him to the lead character who was a stalker. About midway through the first episode, Antonio took it upon himself to clear the plates, so she paused the show while he rattled around in her kitchen, coming back with a glass of red wine for them both.

"Hope you don't mind, I was ready for that drink."

"No, it's fine. Thanks."

"I saw the red roses in the kitchen. Glad you kept this batch."

Julia frowned in confusion. "This batch?"

"Did you think I wouldn't notice the yellow ones at everyone's desk but yours?"

"Oh, that." She had enough shame to duck her head a little. "I tried to give these away too but none of the women would take them after seeing you."

"Damn, Julia you wound my heart."

"You'll survive." She rolled her eyes at him clicking the television back on, but he was stuck on the flowers.

"It's weird since they didn't have a problem taking the others."

"That's because I told them my parents sent those."

"Ms. follow the book Julia lied?"

"I sure did, twice. My business is none of theirs. Well, it wasn't until yesterday." She gave him the side-eye, sipping her wine.

"I'm not even a little bit sorry now since you hurt my feelings giving away my flowers." Antonio declared. "But that was then, and this is now. We're enjoying your stalker show so why don't we focus on that."

"Fine by me, it's the weekend. I want to forget about work completely."

"Amen to that." Antonio co-signed.

When the rest of the episode finished, Julia decided to be charitable and let him pick an actual movie to watch. When the sun set at a quarter past nine on this summer evening, Julia had to confess she was having fun. She was super relaxed, something she hadn't expected when he'd first shown up—he'd been a perfect gentleman, from deeds to words. Julia told herself it was mostly surprise and not disappointment when he didn't make a move on her. No sooner had she thought it than Antonio was sliding closer until their shoulders touched.

"So I was thinking..."

"Oh boy, are you sure you want to do that?"

"You do know I do it daily right? Thinking that is, I help make other folks rich and myself a nice chunk of change along the way."

"A man that's good with money *is* a plus." She teased.

"Indeed. So as I mentioned yesterday I supplied you with two great orgasms yet I only got a solitary one." Antonio's voice was sad as if he'd been cheated out of a great gift.

"You are full of shit." Julia nudged him with her shoulder, biting her lip so she wouldn't laugh.

"No, I'm just a man pointing out a discrepancy with the numbers. Now I know due to your profession *you* probably hate discrepancies even more than I do. I just figured I'd give you a chance to rectify that. You're here, I'm here...would be the perfect time to even the balance sheet."

Julia turned to look at him, their faces only a few inches apart. Focusing on his delectable lips before going up to his laughing eyes. She reached out putting a hand on his leg, watching the laughter fade into desire.

"You're right, I don't like when things don't add up so I'll give you a hand job." Turning more fully toward him she palmed his dick through his pants. "Will that work for you?"

"Hmmm, maybe. Keep going and I'll tell you in a few minutes."

Julia couldn't help it this time, she laughed. Massaging him through his pants until she could feel him growing hard, all the while his hand played with the hair at the nape of her neck. But when her fingers walked their way up to his zipper he stilled her hand.

"What's wrong?"

"I know I'm going to kick myself for this later, but I'm good."

"You're good...as in you want me to stop?"

Antonio's voice was pained when he answered. "Yes, unbelievably that's what I'm saying."

"Why?" She sounded angry about it, even to her own ears.

"It's not you. The more you got going I just started having flashbacks. Reminded me of my youth. Most of the girls in my neighborhood were Catholic. They would hand out handjobs like old ladies hand out hard candy in church. Trying to get *anything* else was like pulling teeth. Picture it, handjobs from eighth grade and up. Every once in a while you might get a blow job."

"Bet you didn't get tired of *those*."

Antonio only grinned. "Uhh no, can't say that I did. But those damn handjobs drove me crazy. Took me til the end of my junior year to lose my virginity!"

"One of the catholic girls finally put out?" Julia was strangely invested in the story.

"Hell no!" He still sounded irritated by that fact. "I finally wised up and found a sweet, Baptist girl that I didn't have to propose to just to see her breasts."

"I...don't even know what to say to that." Julia got out around laughter.

"I should have asked you this before, are you religious?"

"No, I went with my mom to church sometimes, and a few times to vacation bible school during summers. But neither parent was heavy into religion. Why? Are you saying if I was you wouldn't have pursued me? If so, I need to start wearing my cross again."

"Can't you tell I'm traumatized? Those are the formative years in a horny, young boy's life." He swooped in for a tender kiss. "Besides, if you were religious I would have made an exception."

"I'm flattered." She murmured against his lips.

"I'm still horny, though I'm no longer a boy Julia."

She grabbed his cock again and shook her head. "No, you're definitely not."

This time she kissed *him* and not softly either. Pressing her body against his until they lay on the sofa, rolling and fooling around. But they didn't stay there long, making it to an actual bed this time. Where they did all sorts of things that young Antonio only dreamed of.

# Chapter Eight

Finishing a few housekeeping things after the girls-only meeting, the ladies hurried to lock up.

"Hey, what do you say we head to a late lunch?" Mika threw out, shoving her unruly hair behind her ears."

"I'm in, it's been a while with all four of us." Andrea agreed.

"And sadly it's going to be longer." Kimberly said dourly. "I have something I have to do, sorry guys."

"You suck." Mika groused before turning to Julia. "What about you?"

"Yeah I'm in, I can spare an hour."

Arriving at the spot Andrea picked they got their food in short order. Julia let her mind wander as the other ladies talked. When they had first started the center on a hope and a prayer, they'd often gone out to eat after a meeting. Using the time to discuss the program, or how to reach a particular girl. But in the last couple of years so much had changed.

The women squeezed in time for the center between high-pressure jobs, and now for some of them husbands. If Julia blinked too long one of them would be having kids next. God, she should cross herself for even having that thought without clarifying it to say, "one of the two married women". Julia was sure Kimberly wasn't looking for a miscellaneous kid and *she* sure as hell wasn't.

"Earth to Julia, are you okay? You look like you've seen a ghost."

"Sorry, thinking about something that creeped me out. What did I miss while I was in my own head."

"We were talking about how apparently Antonio is dating someone." Mika caught her up.

"I'm sorry, what now?"

"And now you look like you're going to be sick." Andrea, always the mother-hen asked. "Are you sure you're okay?"

"I'm fine." Julia waved away the concern. "Back to this rumor, how do you know he's dating anyone?"

"Mika was saying how she overheard Robert giving Antonio the flower shop information a couple of weeks ago." Andrea explained. "You know the one Robert used to win her over. Must have been someone Antonio wanted to impress."

"I tried to get Robert to tell me who the lucky woman was." Mika wiggled her eyebrows. "He said he didn't know. That it was news to him if Antonio was dating anyone. He did say it sounded like Antonio was trying to get back into the woman's good graces. I think I'm a little jealous he's moved on from the crush        he        had        on        me."

"Well, you shouldn't be." At her tone, the women looked at her funny and Julia hurried to clean it up. "I mean...since you have the man of your dreams."

"Ha, he wasn't the man of my dreams, but he sure turned into it." Mika ruminated. "I think it's sweet Antonio may be on track to be the same for someone else."

"He's   nowhere   near   ready   to   settle   down." Julia mumbled to herself.

"What did you say?" Andrea asked. "Never mind, has he mentioned anyone to you?"

"Me?" Julia's eyes jerked up, pinging between the two women. "Why would he mention who he's dating to me?"

Andrea shrugged. "I don't know, I've seen you talking more lately. You seem friendlier. Which is good since I always got the feeling you didn't like him."

"I wouldn't call it dislike. I just never thought we had much in common."

When the other two women looked at each other for a long moment and then back, Julia knew she'd said too much by saying too little.

"Sis, you're not jealous over Antonio's mystery boo are you?" Mika teased.

"Of course not, I have zero reason to be." She looked off to the side before turning back.

"You have zero reason because you're not interested, or..." Andrea trailed off.

And Mika picked up the thought. "Or because *you're* the mystery boo."

Julia jerked, she hadn't seen that one coming. When her friends started hollering with surprise and shock, she threw her hands up in surrender.

"Damn you Mika, you got me to tell on myself. Assuming he's not giving flowers to women left and right, the flowers were for me. And before either of you ask, yes I've slept with him. Jesus, I should have known you'd find out eventually." Julia threw down her fork. "For the record Andrea, this is all your fault."

"What did I do? I wasn't there when you slept with him!" Andrea exclaimed, choking over laughter.

"Because you had to go fall in love and marry your perfect Cam. If you hadn't done that Mika wouldn't have met her dream man Robert. Then *she* wouldn't have had a wedding and *I* wouldn't have met Antonio. Which means I wouldn't have slept with him either."

They started laughing even harder, to the point folks looked their way and Julia flipped them the finger.

"It's not funny. I was trying to ignore him but he got someone he knows at my job to let him in. The man walked the second set of flowers right up to my desk. I was mortified!"

"Aww! That's sweet." Mika squealed.

"No. What it was, was inappropriate."

"I just want to point out real quick." Andrea interrupted. "That if he knew someone in your office then you may have met him at some point anyway. So I want it noted it's not my fault you met him *or* slept with him."

"I don't know why sleeping with the man is such a bad thing. Antonio is a great guy. I bet he's a great lover too."

Julia neither confirmed or denied Mika's assertion. Instead, she stated her case.

"He's flashy. The whole flower thing was another way for him to show off, make a spectacle. Even to have a little fun he's not the type I should play with."

"Guess it's good it was a one-time thing." Andrea lost her joking tone when she saw Julia's eyes shift away again. "Or...are you just regretting that you didn't keep it to a single time."

"Bingo, I'm kicking myself for even letting it happen once, much less again."

Andrea tried to keep her voice neutral. "Why not just enjoy it? It's been what, about nine months since your last real relationship ended. You're due to just play the field."

"I'm surprised to hear that advice from you, sounds like something Mika would say." Julia glanced at the unusually quiet woman who was busy eating a salad.

"I know." Andrea sighed. "I just feel like you were pretty hurt last time when it didn't work out with Jordan."

"I was with him for over half a year, why wouldn't I be hurt by our split."

"I'm sure you were hurt, but you didn't love him." Mika finally spoke up.

"Excuse me?" Julia whipped her neck around. "What the hell do you mean by that?"

"Exactly what I said. You were with him to be with somebody. There's nothing wrong with that, we've all done it—but you didn't love him."

"Mika maybe you should keep your thoughts to yourself." Andrea warned.

"Oh, we're doing honesty today huh?" Julia's anger flared up and left just as quickly, though she pushed her plate away.

"Yes, we are." Mika confirmed. "And if you're not going to eat your fries can I have them?"

Julia slid them Mika's way.

"I'm so sorry Julia, ignore Mika. You don't have to talk about anything you don't want to."

"Don't apologize for me!" Mika scowled. "You know I hate when people do that."

"It's okay Andrea, she's annoying and in this case a bit insensitive...but Mika's also right."

"I wasn't trying to be an ass, honest." Mika sat back in her seat. "And I guess my observation is a little late. I should have said something while you guys were dating."

"No, you shouldn't have. I probably would have straight cussed you out then." Julia assured her with a small smile. "I've psychoanalyzed myself a few times since the breakup. I loved him, but I wasn't *in* love with him."

When Mika went to gloat, Julia shut her down with a severe look.

"This is already embarrassing so I want you guys to listen. You know I started dating him not long after we got back from your wedding. Jordan was nice and *is* a good guy, just not the guy for me. But I convinced myself he was after seeing how happy Andrea and Cam were, then taking part in that absolutely fairytale wedding with you and Robert. I guess I just wanted my own happy ending."

"Julia...." When Andrea reached out a hand Julia gave it a quick squeeze before continuing.

"Don't either of you dare apologize for being happy. I'm so glad you've found real love, seriously you both deserve it. But I stayed with Jordan so long because I thought one day I'd wake up and magically be in love. Which didn't happen, and when it was clear *he* was in love I had to break it off. Couldn't let him get more invested because I knew I'd never get there with him. I was just pretending, hoping the "fake it til you make it" rule applied to romance as well."

"I know you said not to say it, but I'm still sorry our joy made you feel like that."

"Oh, Andrea don't! That's life, plus time really made me feel that way. Our mid-thirties are directly around the corner. I have a mother who looks at me sadly though she's sweet and never says anything. My dad is great, tells me none of these asswipes are good enough for me."

"I always liked your dad." Mika smiled.

"Yeah, I like him a lot myself."

"I think you might like Antonio a lot too if you gave him a chance." Mika implored softly.

"As a clearly defined *friend* with benefits." Andrea tacked on. "You don't have to fall in love to have companionship. Besides from what I can see, looking for love is the surest way *not* to find it. Love happens when you're least expecting it."

"That's exactly what I'm afraid of." Julia muttered before digging back into what was left of her food.

\* \* \*

Antonio was having his own talk the next week, as he and Robert were grabbing a quick meal out. There was a lot going on in the office so they couldn't take their leisurely time today, when near the end of the meal Robert hit him with a comment.

"I'm a little disappointed in you Tone, falling for the old 'quiet and shy' trick."

"What are you talking about?" Antonio asked, confused. Wondering how they'd gone from chatting it up about sports to this cryptic comment.

"Mika told me who those flowers were for. You're playing with fire with that one." Robert counseled him shrewdly.

"You got it all wrong, I knew going in she was neither shy nor quiet. Besides, I'm just enjoying a nice woman's company. Uhh...but what else did Mika say?"

"Nothing, and even if she had that would be protected by the marriage code."

"No shit, there's a marriage code?"

"Yeah, it's a huge damn book of codes that no one tells you about beforehand." Robert scowled. "Also stop trying to change the subject. If you're just having fun, why the flowers? Why would you care if you messed up?"

"I didn't mess up, more like I hit the wrong note. I wanted to smooth things over is all, just in case we decided to keep playing together. Julia is already a bit standoffish, I was trying to keep everything friendly."

"Yeah okay, so you're not chasing?"

Antonio rolled the glass in his hand, considering before he responded.

"I was chasing, then I caught her, and now...I'm playing it by ear. I think we both are. We're just hanging out, no harm no foul. Overall, she barely gives me the time of day."

"Ahhh but see that's the trick." Robert waved a finger back and forth. "They like making you think they're not interested. Makes it harder to see the trap when they spring it."

"I don't think she's playing games. I think she likes what I have in my pants and who wouldn't." Antonio said slyly. "*But*, I don't think she *likes* that she likes it, if you get my drift?"

"I do, Mika was similar. She hated that she was attracted to me." Robert remembered. "Now, a man can't get a moment's rest."

"Don't even try to front." Antonio grinned, tossing the amount of the bill and a healthy tip on the table. "Your wife has your nose wide open, and you love every minute of it."

Robert held out for a few seconds, his expression stern before breaking out in a wide smile. "Well, if *you're* not careful your ass will be just like me, nose split side to side."

# Chapter Nine

Getting great sex on the regular must be making Julia lose her brain cells. Today she had let Antonio convince her that it wasn't a big deal to ride into the center meeting together, since he had spent the night at her house Friday after work. They were having the joint meeting at the end of August and for the ladies it would be her, Andrea and the teacher Angela who was volunteering, for the guys it was Antonio, Darrell, and Cam.

"I never should have listened to you."

"Relax already, I'm giving you a ride not sexing you down in the main room. It was the most convenient thing to do. Besides, I wasn't aware we were hiding anything, your girls already know anyway."

"How do you know that? And does that mean you've run your mouth to all the men?"

"Of course I didn't, but did you really think once Andrea and Mika knew that Robert wouldn't? You know I'm tight with him. I am allowed to have a friend right, or is that only for women?"

"Whatever. I guess it doesn't matter, but I'd appreciate you not volunteering the information to anyone not currently in the know."

"Tell you what, I'll even lie if they directly ask. Will that make you happy?" Antonio snapped.

"No." She said carefully. "I don't want you to lie."

Julia could tell she had hit a nerve, his lips were tight and so were his hands on the wheel. She placed a hand on his knee and squeezed.

"I'm sorry if it sounded like I had a major problem with us. We've decided to have our friendship, we're adults and *I* for one don't have to explain anything to anyone. I just like my privacy."

Antonio briefly patted her hand. "I understand this about you and I've learned my lesson. I get it. What we do or don't do is between you and me. But a friend talking to another is allowed right?"

"Of course, it is."

"Good!" Antonio said cheerfully moving on to another subject. "I'm taking you to lunch after this."

"You don't have to do that."

"But I am anyway. I'm going to give you a homestyle meal that you're going to love!"

"Really? Well, I can't think of a reason I should pass that up. Just remember I need to get home no later than four. I really should put in a couple of hours of work."

"Won't be a problem. Where we're going the service is great. We should be in and out within an hour and a half tops."

"Sounds like you've eaten at this place a lot."

Antonio laughed. "Many, many times. Don't worry I know the chef personally, the food will be delicious."

"You seem to have a lot of *in's* with people." Julia teased. "Are you sure you're not Italian?"

"Ohhh you wound my pride!"

\* \* \*

The meeting went by quickly, both sets of kids getting better at interacting and being themselves around the other. Thankfully, it wasn't like pulling teeth to get them to talk or interact anymore. Noon came and they ushered the kids out to waiting rides, or so they could wait for the bus. She and Antonio volunteered to wait until all the kids were off safely, so he went out to shoot the shit and noticed Corey and Matias off to the side having what looked like a disagreement. Going over he was fed the usual line of "everything is cool" which it obviously wasn't. Antonio told Corey to go wait with the others, while he addressed Matias privately.

"Talk to me, what's up?"

"Man nothing, I was telling him I was cool and he kept trying to push something on me."

Antonio frowned then reminded himself not to jump to conclusions. "Push what exactly?"

"I'd rather not talk about it."

"Okay, but you aren't getting on that bus until you do and it's coming any minute."

"I don't care, I planned to walk home anyway."

"Not on my watch." Antonio clamped a hand on his shoulder. "Look spit it out, so we both can get out of here, I've got places to go. Why were you planning to walk home and what were you and Corey discussing?"

"Fine, if you gotta know. I don't have enough money for the bus. Corey was trying to cover me but I don't like to owe nobody *nothing*, so I'm going to walk. Is that cool with you."

"No, it's not." Antonio waved the other kids off as the D-Dot bus pulled up. "Are you telling me you came today *knowing* you wouldn't have a way back and that you'd have to walk what...ten to twelve miles home?"

"Yeah, so what?" Matias's voice was defensive. "I didn't want to miss a day. Ya'll was preaching to us about keeping your word and your responsibilities. That's what I was trying to do. Plus walking isn't that big of a deal, I don't have shit else to do today."

"Watch the mouth." Antonio said sternly.

They both just looked at each other before Matias grudgingly apologized. "Sorry, now if that's it, I need to get going."

"Glad to see you were listening when we talk, but it feels like you don't remember the lesson on brotherhood. Corey was trying to help you out, and you really misunderstood the lesson if you think I'm going to walk off and let you fend for yourself."

"What do you expect me to think? You stood here and let the bus go, didn't give me any money did you?"

"No, because you already refused to take money from another brother. But what I will do is give you a ride."

Just then Julia came out checking the door behind her. "Are you ready to go?"

"Yeah, we're coming." He slung an arm around Matias's shoulder as they headed to his car."

"You and Ms. J a thing?"

"We're friends and that's Ms. Julia to you. Mind your business and get in the car."

"Sweet ride!"

"Yeah, I know. Now hop in the back, I told you I had places to go."

* * *

"I'm glad to see we have a chaperone." Julia joked quietly to Antonio.

"What? You don't trust me yet?"

"Not as far as I can throw you." Julia grinned.

"How about if Matias comes to lunch with us, would you feel more comfortable then?"

"Don't be ridiculous."

But Antonio was already calling into the back seat. "Yo, are you hungry?"

"I could eat." The teenager replied quickly.

"See, it's decided." He threw another quick glance at the boy. "Text your parents to let them know."

Matias shook his head in derision. "They won't care."

"Text them anyway if you want to get this grub." Antonio caught the boy's eyes in the rearview mirror. "Remember we talked about doing the right thing even when other people don't. You can't control your parents' actions, only your own."

"Fine man whatever, hope we get there soon, I'm hungry."

Antonio watched as he texted *someone* as they continued on their way. A few minutes went by before Matias spoke up again.

"Aww man, I thought you promised me some food! Look, you can check, I texted my folks. Why are you taking me home?"

"I'm not, chill out."

"Then why are we only a few blocks from my crib?"

"You and Julia have zero faith in me, just trust me."

Not long after, Antonio pulled into the driveway of a neat, trimmed yard of a bright yellow ranch home. "I promised Ms. Julia a homestyle lunch and that's what we're having."

"Yes homestyle, not a *home meal*." Julia said warily. "Who's house is this?"

"You'll have to get out of the car and see."

Julia flipped down the visor to check her hair, which she was wearing natural today, her soft waves flowing freely. All because when they'd gotten out of the shower Antonio said he loved seeing her hair like that. Now he was taking her to meet random people—great. They all hopped out the car, but Matias couldn't let it go.

"Who do you know in my neighborhood?"

"I'm older than you, so that would make it *my* neighborhood." Antonio retorted.

Right then the door opened and an excited woman stepped out. "You made it! And you brought me guests!"

"Matias and Julia meet my madre."

# Chapter Ten

Was the man crazy bringing her to his mother's house! Julia could kill him for this, plus it looked like he was springing the visit on both women. For her part, if she had known she definitely wouldn't have come. But she was here now and being warmly welcomed inside.

"Antonio said he was bringing a friend, I didn't know it would be a very pretty lady. Apologies for my house, if I would have known I'd have straightened up."

Julia took a glance around and pressed her lips tight not to laugh. The house was spotless.

"Mrs. Alvarez, your house is lovely and not a thing looks out of place. I wish I could keep mine this put together."

Camila beamed. "Ahhh beautiful and polite! And who is this handsome young man, is this your son?"

"No Julia doesn't have any children. This is one of our kids that we mentor down at the center I told you about. He lives close by and I was giving him a ride home. Figured I'd give him the best meal of his life as well. You don't mind do you?"

"Not at all, I have enough. Sit, sit, everything is ready, I just have to bring it out. Antonio put out another place setting, your brother is coming."

"You didn't tell me that mamá."

Camila tsked at him. "Well, I guess we surprised each other didn't we."

"Do you need some help?" Julia offered, stifling another laugh.

"No, but I'll take the female company, follow me."

As the two women left, Antonio fixed the table while Matias started looking at the family photos on the shelves.

"Yo man, is this you? You all snaggle-toothed!"

"Yeah, so what. Did you think I was never a kid or something? That's me and Ricardo, my older brother."

Matias had moved on and picked up another frame, a family portrait. "This your old man? Where's he now? Did he dip?"

"That's my father and no he didn't leave. He died when I was ten, but he was a good man until he left this earth."

"Sorry, I didn't mean anything by it."

Antonio gave the teen a quick pat on the shoulder. "It's cool." The front door opening interrupted anything else he might say.

"Hey, Ricardo." Antonio muttered. His mother had gotten him good, she knew he avoided spending time with his brother when he could.

"Oh...what do we have here? Antonio is gracing us with his presence?"

"Look man don't start. I came to have a meal with mamá and some friends."

"What you really mean is you came to mooch her food."

"Excuse me, but your mother says it's time to eat."

Antonio was thankful Julia interrupted before he forgot to be an example for Matias and cuss his brother out.

\*

The first fifteen minutes of lunch Antonio let the conversation flow around him, while he worked to get the temper he rarely displayed under control. Very few folks had the ability to rile him, his brother was one such person. People would have thought the two would be closer considering they were all they had growing up, but the brothers viewed life very differently.

While only two years apart, it always felt like their thinking was eons from each other. Ricardo had preferred the path their father had taken of a manual labor worker. He had gone to community college for a trade certification along with an associate degree in business. As the oldest son Ricardo felt the need to help provide asap and that meant he had worked since the age of sixteen, at eighteen he got a job at one of the auto parts companies. Once his certification and degree were complete he landed a job with one of the big three auto plants.

Antonio gave his brother props, he'd worked hard and gotten a promotion twice in the first two years, becoming a supervisor by the age of twenty-two, and now was a director in his department. Meanwhile, Antonio had been on his own journey, opting for a four-year degree in finance. While he'd worked in high school too, his focus had been on saving for school, though of course he'd helped out in the house also. His brother thought was he was "wasting time with school when he could be making real money" but Ricardo did support him in his own way.

His brother had paid for his college books each and every semester through graduation—though Antonio didn't find out until after the fact. His brother had funneled the money through their mother knowing he would never take it directly from him. The differences didn't stop there though, as Ricardo had found a woman of his dreams and gotten married by twenty-five. It had been a shock he'd actually waited three years before having his first child. Now, the man had two bambino's running around his large suburban home.

Money wasn't a problem for either of them, but how they made it was. Antonio was everything Ricardo wasn't. Single, childless and he'd never had to pick up anything heavier than a pin or a shirt on a hanger. For whatever reason they just didn't rub along well, never able to find common ground. It was what it was, not like he could do anything about it after a lifetime of inaction.

Antonio focused back on the conversation and had to admit it was going pretty well. All he'd wanted to do was give Julia a taste of his moms food and he'd ended up with a mentee and his brother around the table. But everyone seemed to be on their best behavior, even Matias. And after an hour his mom was beaming at the young man as they all walked towards the door.

"It was nice meeting you Matias. Since you live close by you should visit me. Check on me since my two grown sons don't have time for me anymore."

Camila waved off their grumbling denials that she was exaggerating and continued on.

"You ever need a meal, you come see me. I always cook too much. I guess a holdover from feeding two greedy and growing boys."

"Thanks Mrs. Alvarez, I might do that. Your food was real good."

"My pleasure, I enjoyed you *and* Julia's company." Turning to the other woman her smile grew even wider. "I hope you can join us again sometime."

Smiling back, Julia neatly sidestepped the question. "I enjoyed myself too. I'm glad I came. Antonio promised me a fantastic meal and you delivered."

"Antonio, do you have a few minutes to spare?"

At Ricardo's question, his mother hurried to fill the gap. "I'll walk them to the car, you two talk."

"What's up?" Antonio asked when the others cleared the room.

"You tell me." Ricardo displayed a rare smile for his brother. "Looks like you're finally growing up."

"What the hell does that mean?"

"It's a good thing, I'm just saying you finally brought a nice woman home to meet Ma and it's about time. She seems smart too. You need to settle down, start a family."

"Man...it's not even like that. She's a friend from the center weren't you listening."

"Yeah okay. You've never brought a *friend* before."

"I've never worked at a center before either, so what's your point." Antonio said exasperated.

"Exactly, you're doing all kinds of mature things. Like I said you're finally growing up." Ricardo slapped him on the back. "I'm proud of you Bro. Maybe I'll actually entrust you with money to set up my kid's college fund now."

# Chapter Eleven

They dropped Matias off literally just three blocks from his mom's house before heading back to her place. Where he was supposed to go home but Julia ended up inviting him in.

"Thought you had work to do?"

"I did, I mean I do but your mom's food has me feeling drowsy. You don't have to stay because I'm suddenly lazy."

"I knew you would love it. My mom seemed to like you as much as you liked her food."

"Mmmn, she was sweet. I'm trying to figure out how she ended up with two knuckleheads like you and your brother."

Antonio laughed, getting comfortable on the couch. "Why do you say that?"

"Please, don't forget I have a sibling too. While you both were on good behavior for your mom, I definitely felt the tension. What's up with that? Ricardo seems nice."

"I wouldn't say we don't get along...it's more like we just stay out of each other's way."

"I guess I understand that." Julia draped her feet in his lap so she could face him as they talked. "My sister and I get along well, but not so well that we were under each other even when she lived in state."

"Me and my brother have entirely different outlooks on life."

"Why haven't you just agreed to disagree, focus on things you *do* have in common?"

"I don't even know *if* we have anything we agree on."

"How do you not know? Are you saying you don't have any type of personal relationship with him?"

Antonio considered. "Yeah, I guess that about sums it up."

"Why? I get butting heads while growing up, but you're both adults now. You have a niece and a nephew, don't you at least want to be close to *them*?"

"I know you're right. I do think about that, but..."

"But what?" Julia pressed.

"I mean he's never really made an overture."

"But neither have you...right?"

"No." He said slowly. "I haven't. You got me, I could do better."

When she just stared at him coolly he continued.

"I should and *will* do better. Are you happy now?"

"Yes, I am. I think *you'll* be happier being closer to the kids *and* your brother. Sibling bonds can be pretty cool."

"For now I'll take your word on it." Antonio grumbled dragging Julia closer by the legs. "Look at you making me a better man. If my brother and I get closer my mother will think you're a saint."

Julia laughed as he lifted her onto his lap.

"Wow, it's that bad between you two?"

"To my mom it is. She'll think you've performed a miracle, and tell me to keep you." He chuckled, nuzzling her neck.

Julia pushed back from his lips, her eyes growing serious as a question inched up her throat. "What are we doing Antonio?"

"I thought that would be obvious, having a little afternoon delight."

"Be serious, I'm talking about *us*. Going out, sleeping with each other, all of it. We've been seeing each other every week, sometimes more than once for almost two months now. What are *we* doing?"

Fuck, Antonio sat up, while she slid off his lap. "Shit Julia, what kind of question is that."

"An honest one."

"What do you want us to be doing?" He flipped it, stalling as his mind struggled to catch up.

"Don't turn this back on me, I asked *you*."

"But you said *we*, so the question applies to us both."

"Antonio, you took me to see your mother for god's sake! I can only pray you don't take every woman you're sleeping with to meet her...do you?"

Antonio looked appalled, "Of course I don't, don't be ridiculous. You're not just a woman I'm sleeping with."

"What am I outside of that? I'm not clear at this point."

"I don't see why not." He was getting a little annoyed. "Didn't we start this with trying to get to know each other? I thought we were becoming friends."

"Okay...I have a decent number of male friends. But none that I've slept with repeatedly, and none of them whose mother I've met."

"So we're friends with sexual benefits. Is that a bad thing? We like each other's company. I enjoy hanging with you, I thought that was clear."

"We're not college kids just passing the time. At least I'm not." Julia pushed her hair behind her ear, frustrated. "I'm not into prolonged "hook-ups". I've enjoyed our time, I won't pretend I haven't. But we're arriving at places together, meals with family and spending weekends with each other. To me, it seems more than just playing it by ear."

"I'm not understanding where this is coming from."

Antonio was honestly confused. In his mind everything was great, they went out, had fun, and could heat up the sheets. Why did she have to make this more complicated than it was?

"Okay, let me break this down. I am not saying we have to be picking out chinaware. I never wanted to be where we're at...but here we are. Are we dating with the intent to build a long-term relationship, or do you only want a friend with benefits situation? I'd like to know so I can decide if I want either one."

Antonio got up to pace. "You don't think it's a little unfair to spring this on me, while you've had time to think about it."

"I've only had the time it took to get to my house, I honestly don't know what is going on which is why I'm asking. Go ahead, take a couple of minutes, but honestly you shouldn't have to think too hard. I want you to say what you mean and feel. Not anything you have to think up."

As the minutes ticked by Julia watched him as he went back and forth, running those skillful hands through that gorgeous silky hair that she enjoyed gripping when they fucked. She had surprised herself by giving him the power to make the choice of where their relationship was going. Then again she didn't have to *agree* with whatever he decided. Julia was trying to take her own advice and let whatever she felt come out, if he ever spoke—her patience was getting short.

"Tell me something Antonio."

Stopping he came over, squatting in front of her before taking her hand. "The first thing that comes to mind is that I don't want this to end. That's me being honest."

"But you don't want this to progress either..."

"*No*, I didn't say that. I'm getting to know you, you're getting to know me. Do I think this can turn into something more, yes I do. Honestly...I didn't set out for that, but I'm open to it."

"Officially dating, not just fooling around because it's something to do? With the belief this may *eventually* be a full-scale relationship, is that fair to say?"

"Yes." He breathed a sigh of relief. "That's what I'm saying and that's what I want to do. Does that work for you right now?"

Julia hesitated a few seconds.

"I'm okay with that. We're officially *trying* to build a relationship, no more no less. With one caveat, that if either one of us finds that 'hey this isn't going anywhere after all' to just say so. No blindsides, no pretending. Also no more hanging with family. While your mother was lovely and the food was mouth-watering, that wasn't cool to throw us together, okay?"

"I'm sorry I did that, especially without asking first."

"Exactly. That's another half a strike, you only have another half-point to go Antonio." She smirked, kissing his forehead. "Get it together."

"Let me get you together instead." Antonio ran his hand between her thighs and once they opened he shifted until he was between them. Pushing the hem of her long sundress up to her waist to see the light blue panties he had watched her put on that morning.

"You don't..."

"Oh, but I do. I still owe you that serving of delight."

And that's what he gave her, removing her underwear to kiss back up to the sweetness between her legs. At the first lap he was lost, her taste was better than any five-star meal he'd ever had. He took his time licking and suckling, so lost that she had to pull his hair to get his attention. Looking up, he saw her panting, eyes unfocused as she softly ran a thumb over his wet lips.

"Come here." She commanded.

He complied, rising and leaning over as she pulled him in, fusing their lips for a fiery kiss. Then her hands were on his pants, grabbing and pulling until she was squeezing his rock-hard cock. His hands went to work too, pulling at his pants as he wanted to feel her skin, needing to be *in* her flesh. As if she could read his mind, she pushed up releasing him, turning on her knees so she was facing the back of the couch.

The one thing they never butted heads over was sex and he had no problem understanding what she wanted from him. Pushing his pants down a bit more he slid inside, pulling Julia tight against him as he rocked into her slick tightness. Trailing kisses up her neck, his hands fondled her breasts in time to his thrusts. When the first light spasm of her inner muscles came Antonio pinched her nipples. Thrilled when her body wrapped around him even more.

And so the cycle continued, her pleasure was his circling as it climbed to its summit. He was starting to speed up and god how she loved it! Julia loved when he fucked her, reveling in it as their moans and groans filled the house. Before she knew it her breath started to hitch and sensations of heat and electricity traveled through her trembling limbs. One of his hands drifted up the front of her neck, the other down between her legs, using the material of the dress to rub against her throbbing clit. She cried out loudly, only for him to silence her by tightening the hand against her throat. Waves of pleasure rushed through her veins at a speed that made her light-headed. As ecstasy claimed her body, her only thought was *she never wanted this to end.*

# Chapter Twelve

Late September found the weather still comfortable in the low seventies, even as evening rolled in. Allowing Julia to have her window down during the drive as her mind thought over the last three weeks. Their relationship had moved up a level after their talk. They had lunch at least once every week, conversations on the phone three to four times in the same period, mostly just to hear each other's voices. Not like before, when they texted only on a Friday to shore up weekend plans.

All the additional time they spent together not tied to fun or sex was enlightening. They were getting to know all the different aspects of each other's personality, which held some surprises along the way. Julia learned he had a soft spot for issues that affected the less fortunate, she hadn't expected that from him. She also got to see how much of a mama's boy he really was, thankfully not in a bad way. Just that he checked in briefly almost every day and made sure she was taken care of. Something he and his brother did alike.

Julia suggested he use that as a way to get closer with Ricardo, and the two did a minor repair to the house together last weekend. Antonio said they'd only argued a little and that his mother loved having them under the same roof for a few hours. Of course, the home-cooked meal they'd gotten in return was more than enough payment. It was a start for the men to form a real bond, just like she and Antonio were doing.

In fact, Julia had finally told her sister about him earlier in the week. She was always wary of mentioning men too soon to family members, they started dreaming of weddings. Her sister especially wanted Julia to pop out a kid so the cousins could grow up together. But all *she* wanted right now was to enjoy the relationship without putting undue pressure on it. Antonio was not only fun but as she'd learned smart, not to mention an overall kind guy. Their physical connection was icing on the cake.

Still, she didn't mind spending this Friday out with Andrea instead of him. Right before the end of the workday, Andrea asked if she wanted to go for dinner. Since Antonio had informed her of a last-minute work issue she figured why not, after he mentioned he wouldn't be free until well after eight. It worked out as she did some extra work before heading out to meet Andrea. Thankfully, Julia was pulling in the lot now, since her rumbling belly wanted some food.

* * *

Julia could always count on Andrea to be on time, so they were hugging in greeting at six on the dot before heading inside. Tonight they were trying a new place that had popped up six months ago. Fairly upscale in decor and prices, but neither woman minded if the food was delicious. The reviews had been awesome, so they might as well try the place before service started going downhill.

The duo walked through the large interior to the back, taking a table on the terrace before placing their order. As always the two didn't lack for conversation, covering mutual shows they watched, work drama, and a number of other topics. They paid their bills after ordering dessert, so when they finished they could just leave out. But right now it was time for more intimate "girl talk".

"Okay, I've held off all night. Tell me, are you and Antonio still a thing?"

Julia's eyes crinkled as a smile played around her lips, enjoying a bite of key lime pie they were sharing. "This is crazy but we're officially dating as of a few weeks ago."

"Get out! That's great!" Andrea exclaimed. "Why aren't you with him instead of me? I know this is the sweetheart phase, you should have told me you had plans."

"I didn't have plans. Not long before you reached out he let me know he had some work that would keep him really late. We decided to meet up tomorrow. You're one to talk, why aren't you home with your *husband*." Julia said the last in a sing-song voice.

"Oh him, he declared it was "guys night" and hijacked Robert. Which was fine by me. I could use a girls night out my damn self."

Amused by her candor, Julia chuckled. As sweet and kind as Cam was he was still a man, so she had no problem believing Andrea needed a break. "Why didn't Mika come out with us then?"

"Her mother got to her first. She was roped into dinner with her folks."

"Yikes, I bet she's enjoying that."

"It's not as bad as it used to be." Andrea shrugged. "Since she's been with Robert the relationship with her mom has gotten much better. Now that she isn't constantly pushing men and marriage at Mika, they get along pretty good."

"Aww, that's great. I think her mother just wanted her to be settled and happy. You know parents worry."

"They do. But let's get back to *you*." Andrea shook her fork in Julia's direction. "So dating huh? Do you think this could get serious?"

"Maybe. But if I'm honest I've always been attracted to Antonio, which is why I tried to stay away."

"You never did explain that part."

"Because I thought he was a grade-A player and that wasn't what I was looking for."

"And now..." Andrea probed.

"I like spending time with him. He makes me happy. I never thought he was a bad person, just that he wasn't the kind of guy a girl should fall for."

Andrea raised an eyebrow. "Are *you* falling?"

"I might be." Julia felt her cheeks heat, a silly grin followed. "It's early, but I can see trusting him with my heart *if* what we have continues."

"Wow girl, good for you! I'm excited about the possibility. You definitely look happy."

"Stop it!"

"What, I'm serious. I don't know what it is, but when a woman is happy it shows. Don't tell me you couldn't tell when Mika and I were falling hard."

"Yeah, it was sickeningly obvious." Julia rolled her eyes. "Which was why I was so envious and went searching for a bit of what you had."

"Well maybe, *just* maybe it's your turn."

Julia tried not to let the idea get her giddy. "Maybe. Let's get out of here, find a place to catch a little music and people watch."

"Since it's just 7:15, I'm down."

Both ladies gathered their stuff and headed for the exit. They'd gone about twenty feet before Andrea stopped her.

"Oh shoot, we forgot to leave the tip."

"Crap...back we go."

"No, I got it. I appreciate you keeping me company, I'll leave enough for both meals. Go ahead, I'll only be a minute."

"Okay, thanks."

*

Julia kept going, glad she had come out to hang. At her age, most friends were married, had kids, or both. Those things made it hard to spend time with other women, so you had to be flexible when an opportunity presented itself. As the door came into sight she started people watching early. Lazily moving her eyes around the establishment, scanning left then right before stopping dead in her tracks. Antonio sat at a table not that far from the entrance, dressed in one of his expensive suits and sitting with a woman dressed just as nice.

Julia's breath caught in her chest, but blinking didn't clear her vision. He was still there—beaming his charismatic smile across the table. For a brief moment she understood the saying "saw red" as rage swept over her. Before she knew it she was moving, and by the time she reached his table all she felt was cold disdain. He looked up a split second before she arrived, his eyes widening in surprise. They got even bigger when she casually knocked the glass of ice water in his lap.

"Sorry, I thought you were someone better than you are."

# Chapter Thirteen

Antonio didn't know what was worse, the shock of the water, hearing her words *or* seeing the disappointment in Julia's eyes. Whichever it was, it closed his throat as he struggled to speak. Then it was too late as Andrea came hurrying up behind Julia, her lips mouthing "what the fuck" at him before she grabbed Julia's hand with a small tug.

"Let's go." Andrea ordered, as the two walked past him and out the restaurant.

"Are you okay?" The sound of his dinner companion's voice startled him back into focus.

"Umm, forgive me. I'll need a few minutes."

Antonio was up, using the high-quality linen napkin to swipe a couple of times at his clothes, then he was out the door.

\*

"What the hell happened?" Andrea demanded as they reached the sidewalk.

"I just lost it when I saw him there with that...*woman*."

"So, you threw a drink on him?"

"Whatever." Julia was pacing in a tight circle. "It's just water and he's lucky I didn't toss it in his face. Let's get the hell out of here."

But they'd barely taken another two steps before Antonio called out.

"Julia, wait!"

82

Julia turned on her heels so fast it was a miracle her ankles held. "You thought it was a good idea to come out here? Are you crazy?"

Catching up with them he held up his hands. "Look, just let me explain."

"The visual of you sitting at that table was pretty self-explanatory."

"Damnit Julia, it's not! Otherwise, you wouldn't have done what you did."

"I don't want to hear anything you have to say right now. Leave me alone!"

"Too bad, because you're going to listen."

Hearing the rising frustration and bite to his tone, Andrea cleared her throat. Annoyed, Antonio tried getting his temper under control.

"Andrea, can you give us a little privacy."

"Don't ask *my* friend to leave! You need to be more concerned with the company *you* keep." Julia snapped.

"Umm, I'll just be over here, out of the street. You two may want to think about doing the same." Saying so Andrea stepped back, pretending to text on her phone.

Antonio tried pulling Julia towards the curb before she jerked away.

"Don't touch me after you lied to me and got caught red-handed."

"I didn't lie to you!"

"Really?" Julia looked incredulous. "That's how you 'work late' huh?"

"Yes it is, she's a VIP client. This was the only-"

"Oh, bullshit Antonio! I should have known you weren't serious about me! You've never even had me over at your place! I was a plaything this entire time and you were to chicken-shit to say so. You just didn't expect me to find out, but I did and I'm done."

"No, you're not." He lowered his voice walking closer without touching her. "You're not done and neither am I. I'm not going to let this be the end of us. Look, we both need to calm down so we can talk."

"I don't want to talk."

"Yes, you do." Staring into her eyes, Antonio tried to make her *hear* him. "Come to my house tomorrow around noon, spend the entire weekend with me, no sex just-"

"You don't *ever* have to worry about getting sex from me again." Julia interjected.

"Fine, we'll talk about this, about anything else you want to discuss. I want this...me and you Julia but you have to want it too. If you show up, I'll know you think we have something worth working out. *I* think we do."

"Whatever Antonio, don't you have to get back to *work*."

"I do, to the client you've made me look extremely unprofessional in front of. Even so, I still hope to see you tomorrow." With one last look at her, then his wet and stained suit, he walked inside.

Julia was a mass of nerves, her thoughts going a mile a minute, to the point she jumped at the feel of Andrea's hand on her shoulder.

"Sorry...are you okay?"

"No." Julia started walking to the car.

"Just tell me what you want to do?" Andrea trailed her.

"If I said I wanted to go out I'd be lying. You shouldn't have to suffer my bad attitude for the rest of tonight anyway. At this point, I just want to go home."

"Understood...are you okay to drive?"

"Of course. I'm mad, not drunk and even that's fading. I'm starting to feel like an idiot."

"Don't do that to yourself. You're human, you had the right to react...to the situation you saw." Andrea chose her words carefully, hesitating but then had to ask. "Are you going to his house tomorrow?"

"I don't know...I mean hell no! I'd be a fool to believe in him again."

They both heard the question in her last words and Andrea gave the best advice she could.

"Know what's worse than being a fool—being heartbroken when you don't have to be. I think you owe it to yourself to get all the facts so you can decide what to do. Just my opinion."

Julia gave her a quick hug. "Thanks, I have a lot of thinking to do."

* * *

Antonio got home a little past nine, and he immediately poured a glass of scotch before promptly drinking half of it. The second thing he did was text Julia his address to the downtown City Park Lofts where he stayed. He didn't add anything else, just the location, not trusting what he would say or what might set her off. Antonio hadn't exaggerated when he said they both needed to calm down—he was royally pissed! How he held it together during their argument and the rest of dinner he didn't know. Now it was all bubbling to the surface.

"Fuck!"

He didn't need this shit, Antonio thought moving towards his bedroom, stripping off the damp suit. Right now he wanted a shower and then the rest of that drink. His Friday had started out like most, busy as folks tried to shore up agreements before the weekend, nothing out of the ordinary. Until late afternoon when he'd been slammed with the need for this last-minute meeting to accommodate a client's schedule.

Ms. Holman was supposed to meet him on Monday to solidify her account but needed to move that up as she was going out of town unexpectedly on Saturday. So he'd hauled ass getting shit together in only a few hours, things he had meant to spend the *entire* weekend finalizing. After letting Julia know of his schedule change, he had thought nothing else of it.

Then *bam!* Everything had blown up!

Who the hell knew Julia would be at the same restaurant, or that he needed to tell her exactly *how* he was working late? And now the relationship high he'd been on for the last three weeks was gone, just like the sweat and dirt of the day was currently going down the drain. The first real relationship in years for him was just starting to settle around his shoulders, and he liked the weight of it. Enjoyed talking to her during the week about mundane things, and getting her viewpoint on minor decisions that came up. Hell, Antonio looked forward to their weekly lunch dates as a way to relax, his stress levels always dropping after time spent with her.

They were becoming real friends, a real couple and he didn't want to see that end. He was into Julia big time, but he also knew he was out of chances. If they couldn't get past this misstep, it would be over for them. It was all in her hands now. But he knew the odds weren't great, as Julia was a proud woman. Nothing he could do, but see if she felt they were worth fighting for.

# Chapter Fourteen

Julia went home and tried to soothe her nerves with tea—that hadn't worked. Next, she tried a little TV thinking a murder mystery would grab her attention—it hadn't. Instead, the only thing that played over and over in her head were the scenes at the restaurant, which *definitely* didn't help her nerves. Regretting the water thing just the "tiniest bit" Julia supposed she could have said her peace without the splash, but doubted it would have felt as satisfying. A lot of things could have gone better, like him not being there with another woman in the first place. By the time she got the text from Antonio she didn't know how to feel.

Her fingers itched to respond for a hot second before she thought better of it. Tomorrow was tomorrow, she would deal with it then. Barely after ten, she traded her hot tea for a hot toddy before finally going to bed. Surprisingly she fell asleep and didn't wake up until eight in the morning, which left her less than four hours to determine what she was going to do about Antonio's invitation.

Deciding to pretend it was like any other Saturday, she had a light breakfast followed by starting her laundry. Once a load was going she decided to hit the treadmill, since she often did her best thinking on it. Only this time she did it out loud, huffing and puffing while jogging lightly.

*"He's out of chances, he doesn't get another one!"*
*"But does he **deserve** one?"*
*"Maybe...maybe not."*

Damn, she was so tired of the maybe's. Andrea was right, she needed more information to know definitively if Antonio was an ass-hole not worth her time, or if she owed the poor man an apology.

* * *

For Antonio, the light of day didn't make anything seem better, it didn't help that he hadn't slept well. The outcome of today was important to him. So while he wasn't feeling particularly hopeful he straightened up the apartment anyway. Luckily he didn't have much to do since he was rarely here. Between long hours at work, mentoring the boys and spending weekends at Julia's he mostly used the place to chill and sleep.

Planning for the best, he placed a lunch order for delivery from her favorite deli. If Julia didn't show he could eat his sorrows away at least. As the morning crept closer to noon, no amount of looking at his phone was going to speed up time or make her ring his bell. When noon arrived—nothing. No text, no call, no knock. It was early but he deserved a drink and not the wine he had chilling for her.

Capping himself at one for now, Antonio refused to get shit-faced this early in the day. Gazing out the window overlooking the city, all he could think about was he might be losing the biggest deal he never knew he needed. The chance for something great might have slipped through his fingers. These angsty thoughts ran through his head until at 12:30 his Ring Doorbell alerted his phone—Julia was outside.

He watched her for a moment as she still hadn't pressed the button, just standing there looking pensive. He could have rushed to the door but he waited, this had to be her choice today, no cajoling from him. Finally, she looked directly at the lens, as if she could feel him watching and pressed the button. Going to open the door Antonio put his phone away, now their fate would be decided.

"I'm late." Julia stated as he filled the doorframe.

"I don't care." He absorbed the sight of her. "I'm just glad you're here. Come in." She looked fantastic to him, in her comfy yet stylish jumpsuit. He wanted a hug but knew he needed to tread lightly.

"No bag?"

Julia met his eyes before answering. "No, I haven't decided if I'm staying."

"That's okay, this is a start."

She looked around his place, an open modern industrial loft that fit him to a tee. "Your place is nice."

"Thanks. Let's take a seat." He led her to the kitchen bar where she gingerly sat on a stool.

"Antonio we-"

"Let's clear this up quickly. You saw me with a new high-profile client. I was supposed to meet with her Monday but she has a last-minute business flight she's catching today. So I stayed late wrapping up the proposal. Since she was scrambling with her own last-minute preparations, I suggested we meet for dinner. Nothing I don't do here or there for other clients, which you know as we've talked about it. That's what you saw Julia."

"But that's not what you *said*." Julia pressed the point.

"I wasn't aware I had to give you details of *how* I was working late." Antonio replied with more bite than he intended.

"Oh, come on! What did you expect me to think?"

His voice was softer this time. "I expected you to trust me and take me at my word."

"Antonio..." His statement made something clench in her chest. "I just saw her and you, and I..."

When she faltered Antonio picked up his phone, pulling up a number. "This is the one and *only* time I'm going to prove my honor to you, so listen carefully." He pressed the key for a video call.

"What are you doing?"

"Calling my client." Antonio said, positioning the phone just enough so Julia wasn't in view though she could peek over the top or side.

"Hello, Ms. Holman."

Julia could see that it was the same woman from last night. At the time her focus had been mostly on Antonio, but now she could see the woman was older than either of them, though she still looked beautiful.

"Afternoon Antonio!"

"Same to you. I just wanted to let you know I'm sending over the final documents right now." Saying so he hit a few keys on his laptop sitting on the counter. "I know you're pressed for time but if you could sign those and send them back before your flight we'll be all set."

"Perfect! I can do that. I have another hour before I need to leave for the airport. I absolutely hate how they make you arrive so early for international flights. A stupid rule that must be followed if I want to get to Italy I suppose."

Julia could see an actual maid bustling in the background as the woman went into several different rooms as she spoke.

"I totally agree with how annoying that is." He chuckled before getting serious again. "I just want to apologize one more time for last night. I appreciate you being so understanding with my...predicament."

"No need. I wish I hadn't needed to rush our business and then none of this would have happened. This unexpected emergency has caused me a headache and you one as well. Again, if there is anything I can do to smooth things over let me know. As a woman, I can understand what your girlfriend was thinking."

"Still, I hate that you had to deal with my personal matter and the entire unprofessionalism of it."

"There is nothing unprofessional about you. I'm very pleased with the level of service I've gotten from your firm and directly from you. No more apologies, you have my eternal thanks for pulling everything together so quickly and making time to accommodate me. I have to run so I can get you those signatures. I look forward to working with a man of your fortitude that goes the extra mile, even when faced with water in his lap."

They shared a laugh at the reference before Antonio wrapped up the call. "Thanks Ms. Holman, I appreciate the kind words. You have a safe flight."

"That's the plan. Ciao."

He clicked off and they stared at each other for a long moment. Julia felt like a fool, a complete idiot. The woman *was* a client, her words of travel irritations and praise of Antonio sounded genuine. Nothing seemed rehearsed or fake to her ears, nor did it look it. The woman had been unruffled as she talked a bit of business if slightly distracted by her upcoming trip. He *had* mentioned that taking clients out was sometimes part of his job. She remembered because he said it didn't bother him like it did some of his co-workers.

So Julia did the only thing she could—apologize profusely.

"I'm *soooo* sorry Antonio." She briefly touched his hand, unsure if she had the right to do so now. "I never wanted to undermine your work reputation, I should have believed you. Regardless of what I thought, I never should have lashed out like that in public. I could have talked to you later if I had doubts. I regret what I did to you."

"I accept your apology."

Julia jolted, surprised by his quick statement. "Just like that?"

"Yep, just like that. Remember I want to squash this, not drag it out to be petty."

"Okay..." It was hard to believe he'd forgiven her that easily for acting a complete ass. But if him flashing his signature smile her way meant anything, he had.

"Now that we're done with that, tell me you have a bag in the car for me to get."

Julia handed him her keys. "It's in the back seat. Thank you, I really appreciate you forgiving me."

Antonio's shoulders sagged with relief. Glad she'd been prepared to spend the weekend in hopes of working this out. He gave her a brief tight hug, whispering in her ear.

"No Julia...thank *you*, for not giving up on us."

# Chapter Fifteen

After Antonio retrieved her bag they enjoyed the lunch he'd ordered. She was touched after seeing it was her favorite and felt even more terrible. But true to his word he seemed to be over her accusations and dramatics of the previous night. Even stating he knew they had more to talk about but wanted to save that for tomorrow, that for right now he just wanted to enjoy the weekend with her. After receiving the signatures he needed, that's exactly what they did.

When lunch was finished he gave her a tour of the 1100 square foot three-bedroom, two-bath loft—dropping her bag off in the main bedroom, still insisting he'd sleep somewhere else. Then they sat around and relaxed, channel surfing and talking until something finally caught their shared attention, though Julia only made it halfway through the program before falling asleep. With the stress of "last night's drama" behind them, it was like her body slumped in exhaustion. When she woke around four-thirty she was cradled against his chest. For a minute she thought he had fallen asleep too, but saw he watching a game on low to be considerate.

Once up, Julia announced she would cook dinner, reviewing his fridge to see what she had to work with. Deciding she needed to pick up a few things to execute her menu, they took a fairly short walk to a small local market to get what was needed. As it was Saturday downtown was busy with folks on bikes, electric scooters, and the vibrancy that the area was known for.

He ended up helping her cook, which almost turned into a food fight, which *did* turn into a kiss. One that was slow and lingering, that made her feel soft, happy and safe. At that moment Julia didn't care he'd said no sex, she just wanted to be with him. But Antonio pulled back, and after eating they rounded out the night watching movies and playing cards. When it was time for bed she tried pulling him into her room anyway.

"You know I'd love too..." Antonio gently kissed her lips before stepping away.

"What's stopping you?"

"Because I have that pesky thing about my word."

Julia let his hand go, sighing. "Yeah, I was hoping you'd forget about that. It's a wonderful trait but it's blocking us from make-up sex."

He only laughed, kissed her on the forehead, and wished her good night. On Sunday morning they woke around ten and Antonio showed out by making perfect crepes before they both settled down with their electronics. Checking in with the outside world since the first time she'd arrived. Antonio on his laptop, while she used her tablet to browse the internet before restarting a book. It wasn't until around two that he walked over and plucked it from her hands.

"Hey!"

"Sorry, but it's time to give me some attention." Antonio pulled her to his side.

"You could give me a little warning."

"I could have." Antonio gave her a little smile that didn't reach his eyes. "I think it's time we have that talk."

"Like I said, you could warn a girl."

Julia cleared her throat nervously, she had pushed the fact they still had "to talk" to the back of her mind, but that didn't mean she wasn't nervous. To the point her mouth was a bit dry, at the same time her palms were wet. Licking her lips she went for it.

"Where do you want to start?"

"I guess with what brought us to this moment. You know when I give my word I keep it, that's important to me. And I thought I'd already proven that to you before last Friday. We decided we were dating, so I just don't understand why you didn't trust me when I said I was working, regardless of what you saw. Everything *is* forgiven, but you didn't even give me the benefit of the doubt—and that hurts. I want to understand the underlying issue here."

"We said we were dating, not that we were exclusive. I thought you had lied to me when I saw you out."

"Wait." His forehead wrinkled in confusion. "If you thought we weren't exclusive that means you wouldn't have the *right* to get mad if I did take another woman out." Antonio stopped her as she went to speak. "And even if we had agreed to non-exclusive dating that has nothing to do with you not believing me. I said I would be working late, not that I'd be out with someone else. We said if anything changed we'd let the other person know, *not* go behind each other's back. I'll ask again, why didn't you trust me to be truthful with you?"

"I don't know." Julia was exasperated at her own logic. "I guess I didn't trust what we were building, that it was too good to be true. Since we first met I've worried there wasn't enough 'in-between' the chemistry for us to work."

"I think there is." Antonio said quickly.

"I agree. Even before the whole official dating thing, I felt it. These last three weeks really made me see how much we do have outside of attraction. We could have something special, which is why I felt so blindsided and jealous when I saw you with someone else."

"Ahhh, I can understand that cariño." He reached for her hand. "I haven't felt like this in a very, *very* long time but I remember jealousy can be irrational."

"Me either, it's scary. I haven't reacted like that over a guy since high school. I mean there I was, literally *just* telling Andrea I may be falling in love with you and-"

Julia broke off, realizing what she had revealed. Both sets of eyes were filled with shock, his at her words, and her's at the fact she'd said it! A bit of his natural playfulness entered his gaze, as he rubbed her hand in comfort.

"Julia Millan, you *might* be falling in love with me?"

"I *am* falling in love with you Antonio, and it scares me." She squeezed his hand. "You scare me, you always have."

"My god woman you do the same to me!" Antonio raised their entwined hands, kissing the back of hers. "I've been too afraid you would never feel the same about me."

"Me!" Julia let out a loud laugh of joy. "I didn't think *you* were the type to fall in love at all. I guess that's stupid as anyone can, I just struggled to picture you settled down. Maybe because we haven't talked about our past relationships. When was your last committed one?"

"About five years ago." Antonio admitted.

"It's been about a year for me."

"The time in between doesn't mean I'm not capable, I'm picky because I take it seriously." Antonio rushed to reassure her. "It takes a special woman to make me want to commit, and that's you. I'm ready to be in a relationship again."

"I want that too, but can we concede we're probably both rusty in the relationship department? You, because it's been forever and me...I haven't fallen so fast for *anyone* before."

"I get it. I've been trying to balance what was a good pace for us to move at. The reason you've never been to my place is because I didn't want to pressure you. *You're* the one that never wanted to come here. Anytime I would say let's meet at my place, or tried to bring you here after a night out—you declined. I figured it was your way of feeling in control of this thing growing between us."

Antonio watched her blink hard, as the realization of the truth sunk in.

"I didn't want to lose you Julia by making a big deal out of it. There's been something inside me from the start that connected to you. It's why I haven't been able to let you go. Even when you told me *very* directly to move on, I couldn't do it. It's why I kept begging for one more chance."

"Well, you do have a certain charm about you when you beg." She teased, the laughing pair leaning in to touch foreheads.

"So that skill will serve me well in our relationship, huh?"

"It won't hurt, that's for sure." Julia stroked his stubbly jaw, he hadn't shaved all weekend. "To be clear, we're together now?"

"Damn straight. As in you, me and no one else. I want to be *crystal* clear this time around because if you thought your jealous side was bad, you definitely don't want to see mine."

"Noted. I feel like we should celebrate this new understanding." She rubbed his thigh with her free hand. "What do you say?"

"Are you asking me to break my word Ms. go by the book?"

"For me, absolutely! I want to make love to my man, in his bed."

"Well now..." He pulled them off the couch. "My job is to make sure my woman is always happy. Let's go close this deal the right way."

When Antonio pulled her in for a tantalizing kiss, their "instant chemistry" sparked like fire to kindling. It would always be a part of what held them together.

# Epilogue

It was about a year from when Antonio walked into the center for the first time and reconnected with Julia, a day he was forever thankful for. The fellas had spent yesterday having their first meeting with their group of boys. But today, Robert and Cam wanted to thank them for the work ahead this upcoming year. Taking them out for dinner, where they now sat in a private room about to chow down and kick it.

"Where's Devin?" Thomas wondered out loud, his brother was running real late.

"Man...." Darrell ran his hand over his head, his face showing concern. "You know he's still not in the right headspace yet, he wasn't in the mood to hang out."

"Ahh, got it." Thomas left it at that, and so did the rest of the men as a palpable moment of silence filled the room.

"Can you believe how quick our first year of mentoring went?" Cam broke the silence.

Robert nodded in agreement "Nope, it went by quick."

"Right. Now it's time to do it again. Gotta keep our little homies on the path to *get right*."

"Hell Darrell! You just 'got right' yourself." Edward teased.

As usual, Darrell was quick to give as good as he got. "Didn't you just *barely* dig yourself out of the doghouse?"

"Too soon my brother, too soon." Edward clutched his chest. The strife he and his wife had gone through was still too fresh to find funny.

"Crazy, we all started falling in love near this time last year." Antonio pointed out, partly to change the subject.

"Speak for yourself." Robert jested. "Cam and I have been known what's up. You slackers just took longer."

The rest of the men rolled their eyes at the two best friends.

"Whatever, I'll admit you may have shown us the way." Darrell acknowledged. "But this deep relationship shit is hard as hell. In the end, you have to navigate that shit on your own."

"I'll toast to that. It can be a wild ride." Thomas lifted his glass while the other men followed suit.

Cam understood that sentiment first hand. The rollercoaster journey with his wife a few years back had been mostly highs. But when their down time came, it had been *extremely* rough. He had enjoyed seeing Antonio plus the King brothers fall hard, empathizing when they'd had their own low points. Shaking his head from that sober thought, he tried to lighten the mood with some teasing.

"Darrell I thought you were cutting down on your cursing?"

"I am! I mean I have. You know my lady doesn't like that shit."

"And yet, here you are still doing it." Edward stated the obvious.

That moved the brothers into one of their normal surface-level arguments so Antonio tuned out, just smiling and shaking his head. The men at this table were brothers, some blood-brothers, others cousins, and some like him and Cam were close friends. He counted himself lucky to be able to lean on, learn from, and give support back to them. Several of the men had helped him as his relationship continued to blossom over this last year with Julia. And if he got his wish these same men would be at his *own* wedding one day.

Assuming he got up the balls to ask *and* that she said yes. The odds were high that both would happen very soon. Antonio had thrown some ideas around with Cam and Robert a month ago on the best way to go about it. He knew he was as ready as he would ever be and was determined to put his plan into action.

"Tone, you seem deep in thought. You okay?"

Antonio looked at Robert on his left. "I'm good. Did I ever thank you for asking me to be in your wedding?"

The two laughed as they knew Antonio had thanked him excessively during the wedding trip. But Robert understood what the "thank you" today was ultimately about. He knew the appreciation a man had in his heart for *whatever, whoever* brought him together with the love of his life.

"You have my brother, and you are most welcome. Now like my annoying cousin," Robert pointed to Darrell. "kept telling me, *don't fuck it up.*"

"I don't intend to." Antonio had no plans on losing the woman in his life, the one now central to his world. They had proven they had something in-between chemistry—they had love.

# Author Note 2

As always thank you for your support. Please review if you enjoyed it! Stay tuned, those King Brothers fall hard and their stories are coming! Until then thanks for reading my character's stories. Catch up if you haven't read Cam, Robert and Brihanna's story yet, which introduces you to the cousins—The King Brothers!

### Running Into You
Not My Type
One Click For Love